THE
WORLD
of DEW

and
Other Stories

BLUE LIGHT BOOKS

THE WORLD of DEW

and

Other Stories

JULIAN MORTIMER SMITH

INDIANA UNIVERSITY PRESS
INDIANA REVIEW

BLUE LIGHT BOOKS

This book is a publication of
Indiana University Press
Office of Scholarly Publishing
Herman B Wells Library 350
1320 East 10th Street
Bloomington, Indiana 47405 USA
iupress.org

Indiana Review
Bloomington, Indiana

Cataloging information is available
from the Library of Congress.

ISBN 978-0-253-05680-1 (paperback)
ISBN 978-0-253-05681-8 (ebook)

Manufactured in the United States of
America

First printing 2021

For Owen

CONTENTS

Contents

THE
WORLD
of DEW

and
Other Stories

Come-from-Aways

COME-FROM-AWAYS THINK IT'S THE TIDE THAT BRINGS THE
wreckage in, but any local child will tell you the truth of the matter.
You can have fifty fine days in a row, and the beaches will be clean and
empty except for the usual haul of rockweed, driftwood, and old plastic
bottles. Fifty fine days, and then there'll come a thick, foggy night of
the sort we do so well around here, and the next morning there it'll
be—a rocket engine from an alien spaceship, or a cracked satellite dish
as big as a bus, half-buried in the sand down on Bartlett's Beach.

I found out that Shauna was pregnant on one of those thick, foggy
nights. She told me over the phone. She said she wanted to come tell
me in person, but her dad was out with the truck. She wasn't crying
or nothing. She just sounded kind of tired and sad. After she finished
speaking, there was a long silence while she waited for me to say something, but I was on the old rotary phone in the kitchen, and my mom
was within easy earshot, and I wouldn't have known what to say anyway. So we both just said goodbye and hung up.

That night, I bundled myself up in coat, hat, and scarf and
trudged through the half-frozen mud down to the wharf, the fog wet
against my cheeks. There's an old dory down in Peter Saulnier's shed
that he gives me the use of sometimes. Last summer, I ran a little
ferry service to Gull Island. You can walk to the island at low tide,
but tourists don't always know that, and if they arrived at high tide,

they would pay me five dollars for the crossing. If they arrived at low tide, on the other hand, they might walk to the island and fall asleep sunbathing, and I would have to go and rescue them when they woke up and found themselves marooned. Those ones would also pay me the five dollars.

I always liked rowing that dory. I did some of my best thinking going back and forth between Gull Island and the beach. There's something simple and clear about the effort of straining at the oars while the waves slap wetly against the sides. There's also something about it that makes me think of sex, and maybe that's why I went and fetched it on the night I found out that Shauna was pregnant.

I opened the shed as quietly as I could, not wanting to wake Peter's dogs, and dragged the dory over the dunes and onto the beach. It was so dark I couldn't even see where the waves began, so I just dragged the boat along the sand until I felt the seawater soaking into my boots. Then I jumped in and began to row.

* * *

The fog brings the wreckage in, and it's the wreckage of a spacefaring civilization. Those are the local facts. There are various theories to explain those facts, and they depend on who's doing the telling.

Joey Outhouse reckons we're an alien dumping ground.

"Just look around you," he'll say if he's pressed and has had a whiff or two of rum. "Imagine looking down on the Earth from space and thinking to yourself, Now, where am I going to throw all my old trash? The shit nobody wants anymore? Well, I'm telling you, boy, those aliens looked down, and they went all around the world, and this was the place they chose. And be honest: Does that surprise you? It don't surprise me one bit. Just look around you!"

But old Bob Piecemate, who's been to college and fancies himself an intellectual, takes a different view on the issue.

"There's always been something special about this area," he says. "We're close to a portal of some sort. Ley lines intersecting and whatnot. That's where the fog comes from. It's no earthly fog. Nobody who's been out in it can claim it is. The portal opens, and the fog flows out of it. And our dimension is like a bridge. And sometimes, while a spacecraft is passing from one dimension to the other, a bit gets caught and breaks off."

* * *

As I rowed through the fog, I thought about the letters of acceptance on the kitchen table and my mom so thrilled that I would be going to college. That was impossible now, of course. I thought about the sort of job I would be able to get in town and knew there were no jobs to be had now that the tourist ferry from Maine was no longer running and no one was buying lobster on account of the recession. I thought about leaving for the city, but I knew that Shauna would want to stay near her family and her church.

This whole town is like Gull Island, I thought. If you stay too long, it becomes impossible to leave. A piece of you catches, and you have to break it off if you want to get away.

I knew after five minutes that I had overshot the island, but I kept rowing anyway, pulling blindly into the fog until even the orange smudge of the lights on Killam's Wharf had disappeared. And then I was alone.

It was a still night, and I felt that I was rowing through a big cold absence. I thought that this must be what it's like to be in outer space, floating through so much nothingness that all the effort you can give won't make a damn bit of difference, because you'll never get where you're going.

It occurred to me that I would be able to see stars if I were in space, but it was too foggy for that. But then, all of a sudden, I *could* see stars, a whole galaxy of them, spread out below me, underneath the water. And they weren't the reflections of stars neither, I can promise you that. Above my head, the fog was still as thick as stew. But below me—far, far below—the stars burned bright and clear.

Even on a still night like that one, the ocean is always moving, but those stars didn't move. They just hung steady, as if the water were nothing but a thin film and I was looking down through it at something beyond.

Well, I stared into that starry, submarine sky for a long while. I stared until my feet had gone numb and I could barely move my muscles, and I knew that I should start rowing for land, or I would freeze to death. But I no longer knew which way land lay. There were no clues to be had out there in the fog.

I curled into a ball and shivered in the bottom of the boat, muscles tensed as if bracing for a blow, as if the cold could be taken on the chin. The fog and saltwater slosh had soaked through my jacket, and I wondered if I should take it off or keep it on. I knew that wearing wet things could do more harm than good. But wasn't that only true for some materials and not others? What was that jacket even made of? I knew that some people get a stupid urge to strip off their clothes when they're hypothermic, so I didn't trust my gut. I kept the coat on.

I couldn't help but think about Shauna being out there with me. Maybe we would both give in to that stupid urge, and strip naked together, out there in the cold. Or maybe it wouldn't have been stupid with another person there. Maybe that would have been the perfect way to share body heat. I couldn't decide.

I used to fantasize about stuff like that, before I had a girlfriend, back when sex was still a foggy shape on the horizon. I would create these scenarios in which me and a girl would have to get naked together. We were hostages, forced to strip at gunpoint, or we were castaways on a desert island and we had to use our clothes as bandages or rope. We would huddle together for warmth, or comfort, or simply because our shelter was too small *not* to huddle together, and then . . .

And then I didn't know what. I don't think I got beyond that until later. And later the circumstances didn't matter.

But this would have been a good one, I thought, even as I lay there shivering and miserable. Me and a girl in a dory, lost in fog, our clothes sopping wet, hypothermia setting in. We would have no choice but to get naked and hold each other close. We would wrap around each other, flesh to flesh. I would feel the heat of her breath on my shoulder, the squash of her breasts against my chest.

* * *

There's a plastic container under the bench at the dory's stern that contains a first aid kit and a flare gun, so I forced myself to sit up and fumble at it, with my numb fingers, until I got it open. I got out the bright orange pistol and loaded a bright orange flare and pointed the pistol skyward. But then I reconsidered. There was nothing but fog up there. It would swallow the flare whole. So I pointed the pistol down at the clear, starry sky beneath the water. I could hardly feel my finger on the trigger, and I fell on my rear end in surprise as the pistol kicked and the bright, noisy blaze splashed into the water.

The flare didn't fizzle and drown as it should have. Instead, it ripped through the film of water and burst out the other side in a mist of saltwater droplets. And then it was burning there on the other side of the sea, a newborn star, messy and furious, falling into the galaxy.

There's no oxygen in space, and fire needs oxygen to burn. I know that much. But that flare kept burning anyway as it fell.

And why not? The other stars burn in vacuum, somehow.

And then there was something else moving down there. I don't know if it followed my flare or if it was coming this way anyway. It was big, and growing bigger by the second. I thought it might have been a whale—but no, its lines were too precise. It was a perfect circle, and it was glowing. It looked like metal, glinting in the starlight.

To this day, I don't know if Joey Outhouse was right and it was a piece of space junk, or if Bob Piecemate was right and it was a spacecraft that got caught in our dimension. But it came spinning through space, up toward the surface of the sea, larger and larger, until it was right below me, just beyond that film of water.

With a great splash, it breached the surface, lifting my dory onto its fuselage. Water streamed over its sleek metal curves as it heaved up and up, finding its equilibrium on the ocean. Even in my boat, I could feel its warmth rising around me, so I crawled out of the dory to press myself against its hot metal flank.

* * *

Peter Saulnier found me the next morning on Bartlett's Beach, lying unconscious in the sand beside the flying saucer. He brought me to the hospital and got me fixed up. I was all right, just a little dehydrated. I don't know how to make sense of it, but that flying saucer had kept me alive with its warmth, and it carried me back to shore. Peter Saulnier never did get his dory back. I felt bad for that.

* * *

Shauna and I built our house from the wreckage of the saucer. It's a strange circular house with low, curving ceilings, a huge domed skylight, and a toilet designed for an alien anatomy. We got Artie Mayfield to pull it up out of the sand with his backhoe and drag it to the spit of land that juts from Gull Island's western edge. We bought the land for a song. Nobody wants to live in a spot so exposed to the weather. But the saucer is sleek and vacuum-tight, so when the winter storms come, we barely notice.

We've started something of a fad in town. Last month, a glittering geodesic dome washed up on the beach, and Joan Grainger claimed it for use as a greenhouse. Shawn Nickerson is using the nose cone of a rocket as a gravel silo, and Dan Smith now powers his house with the solar panels from a wrecked satellite.

There's talk of the ferry service to Maine starting up again, but even without it, we're beginning to get more come-from-aways in town. They come to see the alien wreckage and what we've done with it. They fall in love with the mystery of the place—that and the cheap property—and they stay. Council's even considering a tax break for locals who build stuff with the wreckage.

The folk at Shauna's church say we shouldn't be living in an alien saucer—unwed and with a child at that—but the tourists love it. They come to Gull Island at low tide to look around our place, and some of them put a donation in the box for little Sarah's college fund.

We discussed not having her. We even drove up to a bright, clean clinic in the city, and the doctor described a process called vacuum aspiration. It made me think of the saucer and its alien technologies. But in the end, we had her—awkward and unplanned, like so many of the kids around here. But we're not going to let her stop us. She's never going to be an anchor.

We've both enrolled in correspondence courses, Shauna and I. It's going to be a long, slow slog, but we're going to make it. I know this because we've got Sarah now. She makes everything harder, but she gives us a reason to succeed as well. She makes our effort simple and clear. She's a beacon, wailing in the night, messy and furious, showing us the direction we should be traveling.

I don't know if we're an alien dumping ground, or a bridge between dimensions, or something else entirely. But when the tourists come to see the saucer, they sometimes linger too long and the tide comes in. When that happens, we invite them in for a cup of tea, and Sarah gets to hear tales from all over the world. And we tell them the local stories in return.

We tell them that it's not the tide that brings the wreckage in.

The World of Dew

Our world of dew
is a world of dew indeed;
and yet, and yet...
Kobayashi Issa (1763–1828) (trans. Michael R. Burch)

I never scan the ship before blastoff. I just buckle in and ignite. It's like striking a match. My ship fizzles noisily through Juntavu's atmosphere and then settles into a nice steady burn that consumes mass until there's almost nothing left. That's where I live—that tiny splinter between your fingernails, that fragment, that almost nothing. You would never know I was carrying the exportable goods of an entire world with me, but that's what all those expensive pseudodimensions tucked away in back are for.

When the match burns out, that's it. My fuel is spent, and I'm still barely out of the system. But I've got all the momentum I need. I can ride that stupendous wave of kinetic energy all the way to Arragarra. I'm going well over light speed now, thanks to the zero-space ram affixed to the prow, and there's nothing to slow me down out here in the almighty night.

Only once I'm beyond the intercept threshold of whatever customs officers and law enforcement agencies exist on the planet I've left behind do I scan the ship, pinpoint the rogue heat signature, the carbon dioxide source that shouldn't be there. A blue blip on my monitor, a ghost in the darkness. Hold G8. A stowaway.

There's often a stowaway. The Brotherhood couldn't function without them. We were all stowaways or castaways or runaways at one point. So I go down to the cargo decks with a paralysis pistol and a crowbar. My computer tells me which crate he's in, whispers it right in my ear so as not to alert him. It's a big crate that's supposed to be full of electronic goods. Lots of packaging and shielding. Easy as pie to chuck some of that junk and make a nice, comfy nest for yourself, become invisible to customs and security. But no one's invisible aboard my ship.

I crack it open and point my pistol, pretending to be a mean old space cowboy, but there's no need. He's curled up and out cold, sleeping like a baby. Must have taken some sedatives. Skip the boredom and fear of the wait. Smart kid.

He's barely more than that. Young enough to be my grandson. Actually, my grandson died of old age millennia ago, but you know what I mean. He's maybe eighteen. Shaved head, lean delicate features that will fill out as he ages but that currently make him look fragile and cute and desperate. A tracksuit and rucksack that look military. Maybe a deserter, then. I can sympathize, old hippie that I am. I've had a few deserters from various military and paramilitary and quasi-military outfits over the years. They tend to be good workers but bad company. Usually they ditch after a few runs anyway.

I manhandle the kid onto one of the light-duty stevedores and take him up to Habitation. I check him over with a DiagnosStick—he's fit as a horse—and leave him snoozing on a bunk with a tray of breakfast on the nightstand. I lock the door to his cabin and tell the computer to keep an eye on him, let me know when he wakes up. He can thank me later.

* * *

The *Doctrine Manual of the Intergalactic Brotherhood of Relativity Freighters* states that everyone who comes to us must be given the chance to join up, stowaways included. The past doesn't matter. Water under the bridge, bygones be bygones, time heals all, et cetera. By suppertime of the first day out of port, whatever prison sentences they faced are long since completed, whatever crimes they committed are ancient history, whatever debts they might have left behind have been made negligble by inflation. What matters is who they are now. The Brotherhood is all about clean slates, fresh starts, second chances. The present is all.

You'd be surprised how many bad apples turn good in the Brotherhood—"get their crunch back," as I like to say. We've become something like a religion, and you can sort of see why. The name fits, for a start. Like an order of monks or something. And then there's the bit about being absolved of all your sins. Your sins grow old, wither away, and die, but you stay young thanks to the relativistic effects of FTL travel. And, like a religion, we tend to attract the downtrodden, the desperate, and the just plain crazy. People who want to leave their lives behind. People who want to disappear. People who are legally prohibited from entering a spaceport.

And that's why I never scan our ship before blastoff. Lax security is our recruiting strategy.

* * *

"Morning, sleepyhead," I say, barging in with a cup of tea and some biscuits. "Welcome aboard the *R. F. Wanderlust*. You made it. Congratulations." I speak to him in Freighttongue, but my computer knows how to translate into this kid's dialect.

"You're Brotherhood?" he asks. His voice is dry and croaky. Probably dehydrated from his long sleep. He's sitting on his bunk, clutching his rucksack in front of him like a shield.

"Yes, I'm Brotherhood," I tell him. "You're safe here. Whoever you were running from has forgotten about you by now. It's been a decade already from their frame of reference. And no, I don't want to know who they were or what you did. You're in the Brotherhood now. The present is all that matters." It was what they told me, back when I was in his position. It made me feel better at the time.

They're always running away from something. I just hope it's not a good home or a broken heart or a pregnant girlfriend. Those ones always end up regretting it, and I can't stand whiners.

"The present is all that matters," he repeats after me, as if he understands. But you don't really get to understand until you've lived with it for a while, until you get used to the fact that everyone you have ever met will be dead by suppertime.

He's nervous and suspicious of me, but he takes the tea and gulps it down, wincing at its bitterness.

"I bought that on Arcnor Prime. Supposed to be very good for you. The jungabeasts eat that plant when they get sick. It heals them, apparently."

"How far is that from my . . . from Juntavu?" he asks.

"Oh, just a little stroll. About seventy clicks."

"Light-years?"

I nod.

Then he asks me something that stowaways never ask: "Did you like Juntavu?"

He says it with timid pride, like it was a meal he had cooked for me. Stowaways are always hopelessly self-absorbed, for the first few days, at least—bursting with excitement and relief and melancholy—so his question catches me off guard. It's so mundane, like he's a tour operator.

I used to take tours of all the planets I visited, but I quickly got bored of that. There are only so many Wonders of the Galaxy you can take. These days, I spend most of my shore time in the bar. I'm suddenly embarrassed by that, by the disarming earnestness of this kid's question.

"I didn't really see much of it," I admit. "Just another delivery to me. I wasn't there long."

He nods. "Me neither," he says.

I'm startled by this response. Young people are rarely so conscious of their youth.

* * *

By the ship's clock, it's three weeks from Juntavu to Arragarra. About two days before we hit the system, we send a message to the local Brotherhood offices announcing our arrival. We're only now dropping back down to sub–light speeds, so that's the longest lead time we can give them. Send the message any sooner, and we outrun it, arrive before it does. But two days is enough—it gives them a good six months of dilated time to prepare.

My stowaway's name is John, and I've grown to like him over the last three weeks. I hope he'll stay on. God knows I could use the help. Just a month ago, I had a crew of half a dozen, but they all bailed on Margaretta Alpha to start a commune on the idyllic southern continent, so I've been on my own for the last few runs. I can run this freighter solo, but it's always good to have at least one or two other people around to lighten the load.

John's a nice, quiet kid. Thoughtful and thorough. It's no wonder he wasn't cut out for the army. Armies are all the same. You've got to be gung-ho and hooah and move-with-a-sense-of-urgency. You can't go round thinking about things all the time, and John seems to spend all his time going round thinking about things, which makes him extremely good at stevedore optimization programming. He takes to the interface like an old pro, organizing the cargo into ever-more-efficient configurations that will save us days of unloading time once we land.

He's curious, full of questions, but also humble and self-effacing. I like that mix. He asks me a lot of things I can't answer, like why the two-day/six-month thing happens and how the pseudodimensions work. He also asks me some things I can answer but won't, like why I joined the Brotherhood. But for the most part I answer his questions as best I can, and I have to admit it's good to chat with another human being again, after a month with only the computer for company.

I give him a brief history of the Brotherhood. The standard spiel. We formed to give some modicum of security and continuity to intersystem freighter crews. Help them deal with relativity. Brotherhood institutional culture is engineered to be utterly robust. You never know what society will be like when you arrive at your destination, but you know the Brotherhood will be there for you. The local offices do all the actual buying and selling, thank God. They auction our cargo off to governments and industry, use the proceeds to fill our holds with local goods, and send us on our way. But maybe the Brotherhood's most important function is running the union bars. Every spaceport anywhere in the inhabited universe has one, so no matter what kind of teetotaling nutcase is in charge when you arrive, you know you'll at least be able to get a decent drink.

"You take absolutely anyone as crew?" John asks.

"Yes, but don't worry." I pat the paralysis pistol at my waist. "This is just for show. The ship itself has excellent countermeasures. We get more than our fair share of maniacs, but you have to put a lot of effort into getting into trouble around here."

The other thing I like about John is that he doesn't talk about himself much. Usually by the end of the first week they've spilled it all— why they're here, what they're running from, what they did, their hopes and fears and dreams—despite my insistence that I don't want to hear it. John's not like that. He's polite and shy and keeps to himself mostly, which makes him seem full of potential, undamaged somehow. Not like the cynical outcasts I'm usually stuck with. It's ironic, I guess, but that makes me curious about him.

We cook together. He knows how to cook with the local Juntavan produce, so I send some stevedores to bring up a few crates, and we break them open. He whips up a delicious stew. I help him chop onions and peel the globular bishopfruit that were a staple in his region. He whistles while he cooks, a slow, halting melody that I wouldn't quite describe as tuneless, but almost.

I haven't bothered to cook since Persa died. I've been eating the blandly perfect stuff that the ship spits out instead. I always told Persa I hated it, but really it was just innocuous. After her death, all I wanted was innocuous.

John is down-to-earth and empty of the kind of drama that so many recruits are so full of, and that makes me see my own aversion to cooking as a silly, dramatic gesture. So I tuck into bishopfruit stew, and I tell him about the local cuisines on the various planets I've visited: the sweet curries on Orbiss IV, the sapphire pancakes on Pentafoo, the delicate towers of crystalized sap on Crantak I.

John nods and grins. "I'd like to try that someday."

The last few months, alone on this freighter, I've felt a steadily rising anxiety. A sense that things are approaching an end, somehow. As if I've had time's valves open too wide for too long and the well is about to run dry. John's youth and shy optimism ease that anxiety.

Or to put it another way, I'm a lonely old fool, and I enjoy having young people around.

* * *

Last time I was on Arragarra, it was in a state of violent anarchy. Now, a few millennia later, it's a peaceful techno-utopia, far more advanced than Juntavu was when we left. The Arragarrans aren't going to get that indistinguishable-from-magic tech boost that we bring to some planets, but, nevertheless, they're pleased as punch that we're here. They haven't had freight from Juntavu in over six hundred years, so the universities and museums are drooling over the cultural and artistic goods packed away in holds A through D. Imagine it—six centuries of art, music, literature, drama, television, and film to catch up on. Not to mention the holoshows, mind dances, martial circuses, etch plays, star games, and all the other art forms that just never developed in their space-time shard.

It takes just over a week to unload, our army of stevedores interfacing with their local Brotherhood counterparts, who in turn take the crates to a vast transit terminal, where sleek lev-trains wait to transport the Juntavan exports to the four corners of the world. Sometimes it's airplanes or ships waiting for our freight, sometimes it's zeppelins, or matter displacers, or beasts of burden. Sometimes cargo cults form around Brotherhood offices. Sometimes the locals don't want to play ball and the freight sits languishing in the Brotherhood's infinite warehouses for centuries. But those are all problems for the local office to deal with. The Brotherhood is nothing if not patient—but us freight runners, we're a different breed from the rank and file. We just take whatever they can give us, fuel up, and ignite.

Managing the stevedores is kind of fun. Satisfying. Like Tetris on an epic scale. The planet-sized mess of the cargo holds slowly becomes a vast, clean emptiness. I can't help but think of the ship as a living thing, emptying its lungs of all that stale volume before sucking in fresh, life-giving freight to sustain it on its next long swim through vacuum.

John's a good worker, and we're done ahead of schedule. When I give him shore leave, he explores Contato Freeport, Arragarra's space-trade hub, but I stay and drink at the union bar. It's too easy to have fun in utopian cultures. There's too much temptation to stay, and I made my decision long ago that I would never stay anywhere ever again. So I drink with freight runners from every corner of the universe and every era you care to name.

We speak to one another in Freighttongue, a simple and exceptionally stable language. It's full of redundancies and evidentials and metalinguistic tags that stop it from evolving. When you first learn it, it's endlessly frustrating. Freighttongue was never meant to be spoken. It was designed by Brotherhood computers to act as a kind of linguistic middleman. I say something in my mother tongue, which my ship's software knows how to translate into Freighttongue; then your software knows how to go from Freighttongue to your mother tongue. That's the idea, at least. In practice, in union bars all across the universe, freight runners just speak Freighttongue directly. We don't so much skip the middleman as become him. Living languages are terribly mercurial, changing beyond recognition in the blink of an eye. In all likelihood, each of us is the sole surviving speaker of his or her mother tongue, so why bother with it? At the union bar, we're all exiles, all homesick and free, which is how we like it. Nobody asks you where or when you're from.

We play games. Games are always the same. I've taken crateloads of board games across thousands of light-years and millennia only to discover nearly identical ones at my destination. The dice might have different numbers of sides, be unevenly weighted or asymmetrical, the value of the faces might increase logarithmically rather than linearly, but the basic mechanics—the creation and release of tension, the structure of risk and reward—are always the same, always familiar.

Another thing that's always the same is the news and sports that play on the wall-mounted TVs. Different technologies, of course, but always, when you get down to it, TVs, pure and simple. Momentous events, world-altering discoveries, salacious celebrity gossip, spectacular saves and goals and fouls, all reassuringly squared away in a corner, neatly packaged in a box, predigested, reminding you that serious people are concerning themselves with important things, giving you license to drink and wallow in self-absorption, to not pay attention. And, tomorrow, to leave it all behind without guilt.

The night before blastoff, I sit playing dice with a family of runners. You often see families running freight together. Four or five generations on the same ship. It's a good way to do it, I suppose, as long as you're careful to avoid inbreeding. They bicker and squabble and laugh over the rules, try to teach me secret techniques and ways to cheat. But I'm preoccupied. I miss Persa, as I tend to when I drink. I'm worried about loneliness, worried I'm becoming a bit strange after so long on my own, worried I'm too old to keep going. And I worry about John. I got used to having him around over the last few weeks, and I'm worried he won't come back, that he'll stay on Arragarra. Utopias are notorious for crew defection. As a native Juntavan, he'll easily find work giving the locals the skinny on all these exotic products flooding their planet.

But then I see something different on the TV screen, something the TV is not there for. It's something that shakes me up, something I can't ignore. I get to my feet and tell my computer to translate the broadcast, and my ears are full of talk of conspiracies and aliens and violence. My tablemates protest that we're in the middle of a round, but I ignore them.

There's no disease on Arragarra, no crime. Nobody dies of anything but old age here. There hasn't been an unnatural death in centuries, so they're all in a tizzy over this. It's John. No obvious marks on him, but obviously dead.

They've already put two and two together and linked him with the recent Relativity Freighter landing. I hear my own name more than once. It's the one proper noun my computer never seems to recognize, and it sounds like "Jooshin Jackobs" from the mouth of the newscaster, but I know they're talking about me. They call the Brotherhood a "shadowy organization" that "has long resisted assimilation into the Enlightened All-State," and they speculate on why we might have wanted this man dead. The local Brotherhood media liaison is on hand to give his official "no comment," which the Arragarrans misinterpret as a tacit admission of guilt. The truth is, the only way Brotherhood locals maintain their autonomy and stability is through scrupulous disinterest in planetary affairs.

Everyone dies. We in this bar, more than anyone, know what that means. If John had stayed on Arragarra, he'd have died of old age tomorrow. I've had crew members murdered before. I've had crew members die aboard my ship. Dying people often want to escape their lives, or they believe that FTL travel will prolong their final days, so they join up. You'll outlive your great-grandchildren in the Brotherhood, but you can't outrun death.

And yet. John was healthy and young and earnest, and his death gets to me. My guess is that whatever military outfit he was running from outfitted him with some sort of antidesertion-slash-anticapture mechanism. Like on the shopping trolleys at Brotherhood commissaries. If you take them too far from the store, the wheels lock up. That whole philosophy makes me angry. Willfully destroying something good and useful just because you can't possess it yourself.

I spend the rest of the night in the bar, sober now, drinking tea, unable to sleep, counting down the minutes to blastoff. By breakfast time tomorrow, John's death will be ancient history. Its mystery will have been solved—or not. His grave will be mossy, his plot overgrown. If they even bury their dead here. Don't know and don't care. I just want to get out of here.

In the morning, I will leave this world, and all that has happened will evaporate like morning dew under the hot sun of my ship's engines. The past will become fragile and trivial, vanish along with Arragarra's white giant, its bright rays unable to keep up. And the present will expand and fill the ship, driving out the ghosts.

*   *   *

I wake up on one of the Brotherhood's guest cots, still fully dressed. I don't remember going to bed. I had planned to stay up until blastoff, but I must have changed my mind as sleep became increasingly seductive. Now I'm late.

I stumble into the spartan little bathroom and splash water on my face, trying to speed the process of waking. Only then do I remember John and what happened to him. No time to think about that now.

I quick-march down the corridors of a nondescript residential unit until I find some Brotherhood employees who give me directions to launch control.

There's a woman waiting for me at the launchpad gate, some expensive-looking luggage at her side, a bright smile on her face.

"Captain Jacobs?" she says as she sees me approaching. She shakes my hand. "My name's Kinnya Lanteren. I'm here to join your crew."

I stare at her a moment, blinking stupidly. She's young and fresh faced. And she's pretty, which makes me suspicious. "Do you know what that means?" I ask.

"Of course," she says a little indignantly.

"Then why?" I ask. My own question surprises me. I never ask.

"I thought..."

"Never mind. We're late. Get on board, and keep out of my way. We launch in under five."

"Aye-aye, Cap'n." She salutes and grins cheekily, a defense against my rudeness.

"You're running awfully late," whines launch control into my ear as we sprint up the boarding ramp. "You want us to delay until the next window?"

"No," I say emphatically. "I'm leaving *now*."

I stuff Kinnya into a chair and tell her to strap in; then I cycle the computer through a rough approximation of a launch procedure, skipping all the redundant steps and some of the safety checks. A brief moment to catch my breath, and we're away, gaining altitude with stomach-turning swiftness, blazing into space.

An hour later, I've showered and shaved, emptied my bladder and combed my hair, and John is ancient history. I emerge from my quarters to apologize to Kinnya. I explain things as honestly and fully as I can. I tell her about John, feeling I owe her that much.

"I'm usually more welcoming," I tell her.

"They were all saying you guys did it, back home," she says. "So you didn't?"

"No. He was a soldier, I think. Some sort of delayed execution for desertion."

"That's terrible," says Kinnya, softly.

I shake my head and laugh a little. "You'd think I'd be used to it."

"He was your friend," she says.

"Not really. We only knew each other a few weeks. I hardly knew a thing about him. And yet... I don't know."

"You liked him," she says.

"Yes."

"He was your friend," she says again, firmly.

* * *

Kinnya doesn't spill. Her motivations are opaque to me. I rarely pick up recruits on utopian worlds, but when I do, it's usually boredom that drives them to leave, a facile desire for adventure, a naive romanticization of hardship and struggle. Usually, they're kicking and screaming to go back within a week.

As a rule, I work utopian kids hard. Might as well get used to the harsh realities of the universe, kiddo, because you're out in it now, at the mercy of the almighty night, and this ship ain't half as bad as most of what's out there.

I send Kinnya to trudge around the holds and check on anomalous crates and cargo that the computer doesn't recognize. That stuff all has to be checked against the billion-page manifest. There are powerful search mechanisms, of course, but it's still tedious as hell. She does the work competently and without complaint. She doesn't seem to mind.

I keep to myself mostly and spend my time in exhausting depression, but we meet up for meals, and I find myself telling her about Persa. I'm embarrassed to find myself fishing for sympathy from a pretty young woman, but that doesn't stop me.

"She joined up as crew. She was funny. I mean, she made me laugh, but she was also funny in the other way too. Peculiar. I couldn't figure out why someone like her would leave her home. She came from a good family. She had grown-up children, like me. She was from a decent late-industrial world. I guess I'm drawn to people I can't figure out."

"She must have told you, though, eventually?" says Kinnya.

"No. Never. At first it was a point of pride, I think. I didn't tell her either. We were both stubborn. Later there was some superstition about it. I didn't want to spoil the mystery, thinking that was what we liked about one another. Later still, when I would have told her anything, it just didn't matter anymore. It was enough just to be with her every day. Eighteen years we were together, and I never knew what she was running from."

"John didn't tell you either," Kinnya says.

I'm shocked by this for some reason, and for a brief moment, I find myself very angry that she has said it. It's such a bland and obvious explanation for my current melancholy that I feel stupid for having fallen victim to it, for not having seen it myself. John reminded me of Persa or, more likely, of myself when I met her.

"*You* haven't told me either," I point out. This is meant as an objection to her theory, but I blush when I realize that it sounds like a come-on.

* * *

Andurum is in the middle of a full-fledged world war when we arrive. A couple of surface-to-air missiles are flung at us as we descend, but they're nothing the ship's countermeasures can't handle.

The local rep apologizes when we land, on behalf of the warring factions. "Fucking Custodians of Truth can't tell a Relativity Freighter from a bomber," he laughs, speaking in rough and rapid Freighttongue. "I'm telling you, they were shitting themselves when they realized their mistake. Thought we would refuse them trade privileges. I even strung the ambassador along for a bit, the poor bastard. You should have seen the look on his face."

Old-fashioned trench warfare is the order of the day on Andurum. Ridiculously bloody and bloody ridiculous. Hundreds of millions have died since it began, and for what? To push the front a few miles in one direction or the other. To consume the planet's already strained natural resources at an insane rate. To render vast segments of the population desperate and homeless and hopeless.

"What's going to happen after we unload?" Kinnya asks our first night planetside. We're watching the news on vacuum-tube televisions in the bar. It's all propaganda, of course, but the bloodshed is so pervasive that even the cheery martial music and joyful announcements of major victories can't quite hide the sense of despair. You can see it in the eyes of the newscasters, in their utterly unconvincing optimism.

"After we unload? We're going to get the hell out of here," I tell Kinnya, knowing that's not what she means. This is the kind of delivery I feel most conflicted about. We're the first freighter to have visited the planet in decades. Our cargo is going to revolutionize warfare overnight. The Arragarrans didn't have a military, but that's irrelevant. The most superficial glance at our manifest reveals antigrav skimmers, portable fission reactors, semisentient dronebots, cloaking devices, neural boosters, neural inhibitors, customizable hallucinogens, hypernutrients.

In the best of all possible worlds, the tech boost would render the causes of the conflict moot and bring peace and prosperity to all, but it is far more likely to result in a swift and brutal genocide, conducted by whoever is shrewd enough or lucky enough to purchase those technologies most amenable to weaponization.

"Who decides who gets our stuff?" Kinnya asks. It occurs to me that this must be hard for her to bear, although she doesn't show it. The best her planet has to offer, the pride of Arragarran culture, given over to genocidal maniacs to do with as they please.

"Market forces," I tell her. It must be tough for the local governments too. They're already resource starved, their economies given over almost exclusively to food and weapons—products that are consumed as fast as they are produced. They haven't got much to trade, and yet they can't risk missing the miracle tech that might be lying in our holds. They can't risk their enemies landing the jackpot. So they pay. We'll take a cargo of weapons and food to Knatat, forty light-years away, weapons and food that are desperately needed at the front.

The windows of the bar overlook the Brotherhood's airstrip. Heavy cargo planes land every two or three minutes, delivering payment from each of the warring factions. A truce reigns on Brotherhood soil, the only truly neutral ground on the planet. Farther off, we can see the sprawling refugee camp that has sprung up just outside the perimeter fences—a sea of frightened, displaced people who believe that proximity to the Brotherhood will keep them safe.

Kinnya stares out at the camp, wide eyed. I watch her out of the corner of my eye. I won't take on any more crew here. Security is too tight. The Brotherhood can't take any chances on a world like Andurum. We would be overrun with refugees, infiltrated by spies and saboteurs. Those who try to cross the perimeter are shot on sight. So it'll just be me and Kinnya for another three weeks.

* * *

It's not until all the work is done and we're twelve hours from blastoff that Kinnya's body is found. I'm working late, putting the final touches on launch prep, trying to get it over with before bed because I hate having to do it in the morning. A senior security officer requests entry onto my ship, wanting to talk to me in person.

She's a stern middle-aged woman, her hair done up in a severe bun, her uniform neatly pressed. "Captain Jacobs?" she says. "I am Over-Sergeant Martins, chief of security. I have some upsetting news to deliver. Your companion, Ms. Lanteren, has been found dead."

She pauses, looking me in the eyes with practiced gravitas and patience. She's done this before.

"How?" is all I can manage.

"We were hoping to ask you the same thing, Captain," she says. "There were no external wounds on her body. She will be taken for an autopsy in the infirmary. Do you know of any reason she might have . . . ?"

"Suicide? I don't know," I tell her. "It's possible."

"I understand she came from a very peaceful world," Sergeant Martins says. "Perhaps the shock of seeing war for the first time . . ."

I nod, acknowledging the possibility. "She didn't seem that way, Sergeant."

She nods as well, and we sit in silence for a while.

"There's something else, Captain," she adds once a decent amount of time has passed. "She was found near a Boroca Dominion cargo plane. That in itself is strange. We have an interdiction perimeter around the landing strip and loading bays. She did not have access to that area. We do not believe she could have circumvented our security without the aid of off-world technology. Did she ever have unsupervised access to your cargo?"

"Of course she did." I shrug. "She was crew. And, besides, she came with her own luggage. She was a walk-on."

"I see." Sergeant Martins looks displeased. Then she says what she has come to say. "That's not all, Captain. The pilot of that cargo plane has vanished."

"Vanished," I repeat dumbly.

"We don't know how. We have Verbatim Visual Record devices installed around the runway. We have heat-signature scanners and motion detectors. We etherimage all the planes coming in and out. Again, we suspect that off-world technology facilitated this disappearing act."

It takes me a while to catch her drift. "You think that Kinnya managed to get a cloaking device, or whatever, to this pilot and then he killed her?"

"It doesn't make sense to me either, Captain. But if he managed to smuggle trade goods out of the compound, it could be awkward for us. The Brotherhood's position in this war is extremely delicate. If Arragarran tech falls into the wrong hands, it could jeopardize our neutrality."

I frown at her and shake my head. "Why would she . . . ?"

"We don't know."

After Sergeant Martins has left and I am lying in my bunk, drenched in a numb insomnia, another possibility occurs to me. And the longer I think about it, the more certain I am that Sergeant Martins is wrong, that Kinnya's murderer is close by and waiting.

*　*　*

I worry that Kinnya's mysterious death will delay my launch, but the local bigwigs seem to want me gone. Out of sight, out of mind, and all that. So I launch on schedule, my holds full of war-forged goods, and another mystery death becomes ancient and irrelevant. Or it would, if not for the stowaway in Fragile Goods.

My computer tells me he's stumbling around the hold in the dark, probably looking for a way up to Habitation. I take the lift down, wearing my blindsight goggles, my pistol at my hip, feeling a bit of a badass. He hears my footsteps as I approach and yells into the darkness, "I surrender. I'm unarmed." He's got his hands above his head, but I zap him anyway and cart him off to the brig.

When he can move and speak again, he begins to complain. I'm in my quarters, reading a book, but he knows I'm listening over the ship's comm system. "I don't deserve this. I just wanted out of that fucking war. Why this cell? Why this pain?"

By the time I arrive, he's quiet again, sitting sullenly on his cot. By now, his muscles will have stopped aching. I push a tray of food through the bars, and he grabs it with obvious relief. The poor guy's starving. Between mouthfuls, he mumbles a few words of thanks, but then he starts to complain again. "Can you let me out please, sir? My name's

Fredrick. I'm a good worker. You'll see. I don't like being trapped in a cage like this."

"Why did you kill her?" I say it loud enough to shut him up.

He looks up at me, through the bars, and raises an eyebrow. "Who?"

In response, I raise my pistol. A look of panic comes into his eyes.

"The girl? No, I don't know what happened. She gave me the disguise and then fell to the ground. A heart attack, maybe. I don't know. I didn't have time to check if she was OK."

"You're lying," I tell him. "I want the truth."

"Why?" he asks. There's something different in his voice now, a spark of confidence. "I thought the present is all that matters. I thought you accept anyone as crew."

So he knows Brotherhood doctrine. I lower my pistol slowly. He's right, of course. I should not be asking him these things, but I ask him anyway. "Why did you kill her?"

He doesn't respond. He sits back down on his bunk and closes his eyes. I leave him there and go about my work, worried by my own worry.

Two mysterious deaths in a row. It cannot be anything but coincidence. And yet something nags at me, prevents me from sleeping. I flip on the PA system and listen in on my prisoner. Expecting silence, or snores, I am taken aback to hear a low, almost-tuneless whistling.

Tomorrow I will release him and put him to work.

* * *

Knatat is a lush, underpopulated jungle world. It is a well-functioning anarchy, and the populace has little use for what we have brought. War is an alien concept, as is famine. We unload anyway, into the Brotherhood's pseudodimensional warehouses, and fill our holds with heavy industrial equipment and raw materials that an earlier freighter brought a few months ago—equally unwanted goods.

"They'll need weapons sooner or later," I explain to Fredrick. "Everyone gets round to war eventually."

Fredrick vanishes into the wilderness a day before our departure. The Brotherhood facilities here have no security, and there is no one to stop him. But I am joined by a walk-on—an old woman named Muriel.

She always has a bitter scowl on her face, but she is kind and works hard, and she never tells me why she has joined. She whistles an almost-tune that is becoming increasingly familiar.

Muriel dies on Lorinian a month later. The doctors suspect a heart attack. Lorinian is a feudal-industrial world, where a small aristocracy control the vast majority of the wealth. They buy up our cargo as if it were nothing and sell us extravagant works of art, fine china, pleasure-drugs. A teenage boy smuggles himself onto the ship during loading. He was a servant to one of the noble houses. He disappears into the mazelike streets of Hrall megacity on Pelnan Alpha two weeks later, only to be replaced by a young girl, a surprisingly articulate street urchin named Ramana.

I don't pay much attention to my crew anymore. I leave them to their own devices and spend my time scanning through a hundred billion pages of local history—documents, both physical and electronic, from all the planets I have ever visited. I used to collect histories and encyclopedias as souvenirs in my early days. I loved reading about different cultures, different ways of living and being and thinking, different ways a society could be structured. I stopped reading them before I stopped collecting them. Even now that I've stopped collecting, I still receive briefings from all the planets I visit, documents that the local Brotherhood reps have compiled, appraising me of the current social climate. I mostly use these briefings to help make decisions about shore leave and other matters of security, but now I delve into the background reports and current events—the fluff and padding, as I used to think of it.

I find it on my way to Ekrark's World. It is a piece of history, almost prehistory, almost legend. It came from Kooreen II, in the back pages of a guidebook, uploaded to my computer by a tourism company as part of a welcome package. There is a certain prison on Kooreen, a source of great pride and great shame. It was built during an alien invasion, but after the aliens were driven off, the Kooreenies were forced to inter their own people in this prison. The suffering of those prisoners was so profound and heartbreaking that there has never been a war since on Kooreen. The Kooreenies simply cannot stomach it. The memory of this prison is too much for them to bear.

The guidebook makes much of the prison in its role as a monument to everlasting peace, but it sketches the invasion and the war briefly. It is told simply, almost as a children's story, as something whose veracity is beside the point. It may or may not have happened like that, it seems to say—what matters is what the prison is *now*. I read it and reread it, and then I take my paralysis pistol and go to find my current crewmate.

* * *

I picked her up on Chosslitz, a stifling theocracy. She was a walk-on, but she came in secret, under cover of night. She wore the robes of a priestess of the highest order, but once we were away, she was all too happy to don the overalls of the Brotherhood and make herself useful, whistling that almost-tuneless melody as she worked. Everyone I've picked up since Juntavu has been remarkably willing to work, remarkably talented, unremarkable whistlers.

I find her in the mess, cooking breakfast. "Leave that for now, and follow me," I tell her. She comes without complaint. I take her all the way through Habitation to Embarkation, unlocking the security doors with biometric pass phrases.

"Where are we going?" she asks more than once, but I do not answer.

Finally we reach the crew air lock, and I have to manually override a dozen safety mechanisms to get the interior door open.

"After you." I usher her into the chamber and lock the door behind her. She realizes what is happening before the massive door can close and seal completely, but I have my pistol pointed at her by then, and she hesitates. Then it is too late. She is trapped between two massive vacuum-carbon bulwarks. We can see each other's face through the little window, but our voices have to be transmitted through the computer.

"Let's drop this charade," I say to her.

She stares at me through six inches of plastic, her hands spread against the pane. I imagine that she's trying to work out if I'm bluffing or not.

"Why not the brig again?" she says softly.

"This is safer."

"I trusted you," she says then. It seems an odd thing to say, and I laugh at her.

"I don't trust you. You killed them all. Everyone I've had on board since Juntavu. Since John. Right? Maybe farther back. I don't know how it works."

"They would all be dead by now anyway." Her voice sounds strange and metallic over the comm link. There's an echo in it that wasn't there before.

"This is different."

"How?" she asks. "Why do you care?"

And for a moment I'm stumped. Is it having a murderer as crew? That's nothing new to me. Over the years I've had a wide range of murderers on this ship—some crazy, some just bad. Sometimes I was forced to throw them in the brig and ditch them at our next stop, but there were also those whom I befriended. There was a hitman from Kentish who stayed with me for dozens of runs. He was one of my best workers. So why is this different?

"I'm asking the questions here," I tell her feebly, feeling like a bad cliché. "What are you? Tell me."

She speaks a word that my computer does not know how to translate. Then she shrugs. "We just call ourselves *people*."

"And what do others call you?" I ask. "What do humans call you?"

"Different things," she says. "I have spoken in many tongues in my day. Mind-eaters. Parasites. Doppelgangers. Demons. Possessors."

"The Kooreenies called you Devourers," I tell her, and she nods in acknowledgment. "Were you there?"

"That was where our army was defeated. That was where the Great Starvation occurred. Yes, I was there. Only a few of my people escaped, but I was one of them."

I look at her through the glass, and I see that she is frightened. I try to see a parasitic alien behind the girl's eyes, but I cannot. The human brain is hardwired for face recognition. I cannot see her as anything but a frightened girl.

"The Great Starvation," I say at last. "The prison. The Koreenies had to kill their own people to be rid of you. They had to watch their friends and loved ones die."

"No." Her eyes flash with sudden anger. "They watched *my* people die. *My* friends, *my* loved ones. They watched them starve to death. If we cannot feed, we suffer. And the suffering of my people is a most terrible thing."

"What about the suffering of the Kooreenies?" I ask. I'm angry too now, inexplicably. The war on Kooreen was ancient history even at the time of my visit, millions of years ago. "What about John's suffering?" I add, realizing that this is what I really mean. "What about Kinnya's? And all the people you have fed on since coming aboard my ship?"

"There is something you have to understand," she says. She regains her composure with a visible effort of will, raising her palms to the window in a conciliatory gesture. "I have visited many, many worlds since my time on Kooreen. I have made a study of suffering, in humans and other creatures. I have studied biology and physiology, psychology and neurology, cognitive science and spiritual science. I have learned about these things from the most advanced civilizations, and I have learned different things from the most primitive. I have concluded that the suffering experienced by my people is far greater than anything a human is capable of experiencing. Trillions of times greater."

"Bullshit," I tell her.

"I know it is hard to accept, but it is true," she speaks in a rush now, as if in a panic, as if taking a risk and wanting to get it over with. "Human suffering is a complex and many-faceted thing. It involves nociception, nerve fibers, the limbic system, the cingulate cortex, the hypothalamus. It can be physical, or it can be emotional. It has a cultural dimension, a spiritual dimension, an aesthetic dimension. It can seem agonizing, or it can carry pleasure with it. I know all this. I also know you have opioid receptors and endorphins that limit suffering, that you lose consciousness when your suffering reaches a certain threshold.

"I have lived in many, many human bodies. I have felt pain with human nerves. I have felt torture and heartbreak. I have felt disease, and I have felt grief. I know that your suffering can seem like the most important thing in the universe, but I also know that you are mistaken in thinking this. Human suffering is a faint and meager thing, a surface with no depth. But for my people—our suffering is different. It is far less subtle, far less complex than human suffering. It is blunt and vast and inconceivable. And we only suffer when we are hungry."

She pauses, and again I see fear in her eyes. "And we can only die by starvation." She glances at the outer air-lock door, and I imagine her floating in vacuum, her body slowly radiating heat, drifting inexorably toward the ambient temperature, a hair above absolute zero. And I imagine a conscious being trapped in that icy corpse, growing hungry.

"You eat the minds of your hosts," I say, dumbly. I am horrified and fascinated, angry and curious. I don't know what to believe or what to feel.

"Eat is imprecise," she tells me. "We are nourished by cognition. Some cultures describe us as syncretic personae. We build our own sentience from the sentience of others. But yes, if you like, we eat minds. We eat them, and we excrete them."

"How many? How many people have you killed?"

"Thousands," she says, and I hear something in her voice that I interpret as flippancy. "I have to take a new host every few months. If not, the hunger begins. I have sustained myself for over four hundred years. Only twice have I felt hunger. Just the beginnings, a shadow of what was to come. And both times it was enough . . ."

"Enough for what?"

"Enough to force me to do what was needed to sate my hunger. Things I am not proud of."

I walk away and leave her there in the air lock, and before I switch off my comm link, I hear what sounds like a sob of frustration, quiet and human.

I don't sleep that night. I lie on my bunk thinking about the creature in my air lock. From time to time I switch the comm link back on and listen to her pleading with me for release: "—can drop me at the next world, and I will go and leave you in peace. You can forget about me like you forget about all those you leave behind. I only stayed with you because you didn't seem to care. No, that's not exactly true. I stayed because I could travel from world to world, taking just one life at a time, never staying long enough to arouse suspicion, never risking imprisonment. But I believed that you accepted everyone, no matter what, and that made me—" Click.

Then later: "—always having that at my heels. Never being trusted by anyone. I feel what my host feels. I feel the guilt and the sadness at leaving their families and friends. You must know what that is like. They do not suffer when I possess them. I take their suffering upon myself. It is not easy. I do not enjoy it. But the terror of hunger pushes me on. If I could die in any other way—" Click.

Later still, silence. And in the midst of that silence: "I am often lonely."

I haven't eaten since breakfast, and I am growing hungry myself. I try to imagine that hunger being a trillion times more intense, and I find it impossible, a meaningless exercise. How to even quantify something as subjective as suffering?

And then I imagine taking possession of human bodies and discarding them like sandwich wrappers. I imagine viewing all the suffering of humanity as a trivial, diaphanous thing. I imagine what it is like to kill an innocent person because the alternative is unbearable.

I find all that remarkably easy to imagine.

I open a comm channel to the air lock again. The creature is silent now, perhaps asleep. "Let me tell you about Persa," I say into the silence. "She didn't die. Not quite. She *is* long dead, but I was lying when I told you that she died. She left me. For eighteen years we traveled the stars together, and then one day she had had enough. She disappeared on shore leave and did not return to the ship for launch. She left a note, telling me not to come looking for her. Telling me to launch without her. Telling me she was sorry. It was a suicide note. Maybe she didn't mean it that way, but for me that's what it was. From my frame of reference, she would be dead within days of leaving the planet. From hers, she had the rest of her life ahead of her. We had talked about stopping. About retiring together. But after that, I knew I could never stop."

There is no response, and I do not know if the creature has heard me or not. I don't know why I have told her this.

Later still, I hear a low whistling, and at last, for the first time, I do not hear it as tuneless. Through a slow accumulation, it has become a melody, both ugly and beautiful.

The next morning, I go to the air lock again. The girl is crouched in one corner. There is a pool of urine on the floor. She looks exhausted, and I know she has not slept on that hard floor, under those bright lights, with the stink of piss endlessly circulating in the recycled air.

The World of Dew and Other Stories

She pulls herself to her feet, stiffly, when she sees me at the window, and hobbles over and stares at me with tired, bloodshot eyes.

I don't speak. I don't know why I have come.

"My nervous system is separate from that of my host," she says, the croak of thirst in her voice. "But I still feel its thirst, its pain. If this host body dies, I will still be able to move its muscles. But I hate doing that. You have heard stories of zombies? We have always lived among you."

"Why Kooreen? Why the invasion?" I ask.

There is a long silence before she responds. "We wanted to enslave a planet. We wanted to keep a breeding population enslaved so that we need never go hungry again. We were punished for our hubris."

I turn away in disgust.

"It was wrong," she mumbles. "We were defeated. It is better this way. The diaspora. Each of us alone, taking our hosts suddenly and secretly. They do not suffer. They do not even know."

"John," I say to her. "I liked him a great deal. And Kinnya. And the others too. I liked them."

"You like *me*." She smiles weakly. "They were all me."

I am made angry again by this bait and switch. I feel betrayed.

"Listen," she says. "My personality is the sum of all the people I have inhabited. I remember what it is like to be them. My hosts die, but a part of each of them lives on in me. I kill them, yes, but I give them a kind of immortality as well."

A stab of wild hope—impossible, but also impossible to dismiss. The sense of familiarity about John, the way I felt less anxious around him. His quiet, easy smile. His melancholy. I blurt it out, knowing it is not true: "Persa. You were once Persa. You took her from me. *You* wrote that note, not her."

A look of worry crosses the girl's face, then a look of sadness, of pity.

"No," she says softly, not meeting my eyes.

Something collapses inside me. A shred of hope and dread, calving from my heart.

No, of course not.

I look at this frightened, tired creature before me, this mass-murdering parasite, and I flip the switch that opens the air lock.

* * *

I blast off from Ekrark's World with a cargo of jewels, spices, and perfumes. Ekrark's capital, a magnificent city called Weeming, is a place devoted to reckless hedonism. There are few laws there, but its people have little reason to commit crimes. Everything they could want is at their fingertips. The Devourer could be safe in such a city. Drug overdoses are common and are never investigated. Nobody would notice a mysterious death every few months. But she comes back to the ship on the morning of blastoff in the body of a retired dancer.

We fizzle noisily through the atmosphere and then settle into a nice steady burn, our engines consuming the mass of the ship until there's almost nothing left. Just a splinter between your fingertips.

* * *

Sometimes we are lovers, the Devourer and I, when it possesses a body of the right sex and age. At first this disturbs me, even as it thrills me. It seems a kind of violation, or even necrophilia. But then the Devourer whispers into my ear to keep going, and it no longer matters. The anxiety eases, and I feel, somehow, absolved of my sins.

At other times we are just friends, keeping each other company out here in the almighty night, raging together against the loneliness, washing ourselves clean in a torrent of time, until we can no longer remember what we are running from.

Water under the bridge, bygones be bygones, and time heals all, et cetera.

Amen.

Barb-the-Bomb and the Yesterday Boy

I HAVE A CRUSH ON A BOY FROM YESTERDAY.

He's a small, lean boy about my age. A beggar child. I first see him sitting in a boarded-up doorway in Fumblers Alley. He holds a cloth cap out in front of him, shaking it so that the coins *tink-tink* together. He has a piece of slate with words scratched onto its face: "Spare a thought. Spare a coin. Thank you from yesterday."

It's the *tink-tinking* that catches my attention, but it also catches the attention of a gang of proudscum kids. I've seen them before. They call themselves the Sniders, and their leader is a big ugly kid named Mulligan. As I watch, they muscle right up to the yesterday boy. They dare each other to touch him, and then Mulligan steals the change right out of his hat. The others laugh. The poor yesterday boy doesn't even notice, of course, because that happens today and he's still living yesterday, but he will notice tomorrow.

I tear across the street, all fists and kicks. At school they call me Barb-the-Bomb because of my sudden tempers. I like that nickname. I have to dodge a clattering carriage and a group of properfolk to get to Mulligan and his gang, but I'm fast, and I reach the Sniders before my mother even notices I'm no longer by her side. She starts to scream at the same moment that Mulligan does. Before the rest of the gang realize what's happening, I've punched him twice in the nose and kicked him hard in the shins. He drops his stolen coins and yells a lot of nastiness, and then his gang is upon me. They're bigger and heavier than I am. They pin me to the cobbles and sit on me, force my face into the filth and sewage that fill the gutter. Then Mulligan stamps on my fingers, and it's my turn to scream.

My mother saves me from that one. She beats the Sniders off with the blunt end of her umbrella. They run off swearing revenge and also just swearing. Then my mother hooks the handle of her umbrella around my neck and pulls me to my feet. I choke and splutter while she looks me up and down and inspects my crushed hand, my drenched and stinking dress, my bruised face. She's clearly furious, but she doesn't say anything. That's much scarier than even the worst scolding would have been. She just watches me with her hands on her hips. She wants to know what I hoped to accomplish with my behavior, so I bend down and gather up the scattered coins with my uninjured hand and drop them in the yesterday boy's hat. He won't notice me until tomorrow, but I smile at him anyway and tell him that my name is Barb.

"Don't touch him," my mother warns, "or you might end up when he is." Her voice is sharp and quivers with anger, but there is also a note of sympathy there. Perhaps a part of her understands why I had to do it.

"There's nothing more you can do for him," says my mother. But I'm not so sure. I can come back tomorrow and watch the theft and the fight play out on his face, watch how he reacts when I return his coins. And maybe, if he guesses that I might come back, he'll smile and thank me and tell me his name in return.

And that could be the start of an awkward, blushing something.

The Fumblers Alley Risk Emporium

DESPERATION WAS THE WORST THING YOU COULD BRING TO the Emporium, but there was nowhere else to go. The Emporium was the only place that would have what I was looking for. It *always* had what I was looking for. So I brought my desperation with me, like an albatross around my neck, like a black spot.

You could get it all at the Emporium. But not for money; Mr. Handlesropes didn't operate that way. Sometimes, one of the art addicts who dealt in the alley would come in and offer huge sums of stolen cash for one of his items—a piece of cured human skin bearing a rare tattoo, or the shell of a dodo egg, hand-painted by a prisoner on the day before his execution—but Mr. Handlesropes would just laugh.

"You've got to play the game like everyone else, son," he would say, even if the petitioner were a woman many years his senior.

During the day, the Emporium acted as a gallery of sorts, its display cases overflowing with rare artifacts and curiosities. But if you wanted to possess one of the items that Mr. Handlesropes stocked, you had to wait until closing time, when he would blow out his lanterns and lead you down the narrow twist of a staircase into the cold stone basement, where his balance was set up on a circular bar table.

I was a habitué in the basement of the Emporium. I often came seeking treasures that could not be had anywhere else. But that night was different. I was all atwitch with worry and exhaustion. I hadn't slept in as long as I could remember. I was kept awake by gallons of cheap coffee and the buzz-saw whine of anxiety. Usually there was a sense of excitement when Mr. Handlesropes led the hopefuls down to the basement, but that night I only felt panic and paranoia.

There were three others there that night. Two were regulars—Mama Alphonz-Custer and Dame Prudence Weakforce. I had seen them many times in that cellar, playing for outrageous prizes, risking priceless treasures, losing as often as they won. Sometimes we would meet up afterward to celebrate or commiserate or strategize over pints of Hogtown Peculier at Crobbleknock Tavern. We called our little club the Aficionados. We prided ourselves on being expert at Mr. Handlesropes's game, but we all knew that nobody was truly expert.

The third player that night was a newcomer. A small fox-like man with sharp eyes and a glittering smile. I had never seen him in the Emporium before, but I instantly disliked him. He sat in silence as Dame Weakforce and Mama Alphonz-Custer offered unsolicited advice.

"It's all in the materials," whispered Mama Alphonz-Custer. "Mr. Handlesropes knows how much your wager is worth, and that determines the material of the token, and the weight. You can never get away with trying to cheat him. You've just got to offer him a fair deal, and you'll win every time."

"It's more than that," Dame Weakforce chimed in. "He knows how much your wager is worth to *you*. Or the tokens do, at any rate. And what's more, he knows how much you want the thing you're playing for. You've got to be honest with yourself. What would I give to obtain this tchotchke or that kickshaw? How much would I really be willing to part with?"

The fox-like man smiled and nodded. I shivered and kept silent.

One corner of the cellar was always hidden from view by heavy curtains, but there must have been a piano back there, and a piano player, because once we had all taken our seats, Mr. Handlesropes snapped his fingers and music began. It was a breed of music I had never heard anywhere else, somewhere between a dissonant funeral march and a frantic, stomping ragtime. It worked its way into your dreams, that music. If you listened carefully, you could also sometimes hear a low growl and the clink of chains from behind that curtain. The pianist wasn't human; of that we were certain.

Mr. Handlesropes poured everyone the customary shot of his noisome homemade absinthe and made a toast to the balance, and to Lady Luck, and to the Gentleman of Loss.

And then the game began.

* * *

Mr. Handlesropes's game was simple and strange: each customer in turn would name the object that he or she wanted from the Emporium, and Mr. Handlesropes would produce a circular token from his voluminous pockets with a picture of that object etched into its surface. Mr. Handlesropes knew his inventory with an uncanny precision, and it never took him more than a moment to pull the correct token from his pocket, apparently by feel alone.

The tokens were made out of all sorts of different materials—mahogany, steel, slate, iron, teak, bone, ivory, cardboard, shell—and varied in size and weight quite dramatically. The smallest were the size of small coins or shirt buttons; the largest were the size of your hand with your fingers splayed. Mr. Handlesropes would lay the token on the table in front of him, to the left of the balance.

Next, each customer would name another object—something she was willing to risk in order to gain the object of her desire. And here's what I could never figure out: Mr. Handlesropes would have tokens representing those objects too, each token bearing a precise etching of the object in question. He would pull it from his pocket as quickly as he did those representing his own merchandise and place it before him, to the right of the balance.

I had often wagered things he never could have seen: one time it was an old rocking horse that had belonged to my great-grandfather. He pulled out a token made of wood—and there it was, etched onto the face, the lines filled with dark ink. Not just any rocking horse, but my great-grandfather's rocking horse, complete with missing eye and broken tail.

After the two piles of tokens were lying there on the table, on either side of the balance, the weighing would begin.

Mr. Handlesropes would place the token representing the thing you wanted in one pan of his balance; the token representing the thing you were risking would go in the other pan. If they weighed the same, or thereabouts, you got to keep both, but if the balance tilted to one side or the other, then Mr. Handlesropes got to keep both.

And that was how it worked.

Mr. Handlesropes's stock included wonders from all over the world, things I obsessed over, things I lusted after. There was a heavy skillet with gunpowder mixed into the iron that would pop and spark as you cooked, searing your meat with a thousand tiny explosions, flavoring it with acrid smoke. There was an umbrella with spokes as sharp as razors and grooves to channel rain or other liquids into a small reservoir inside the handle. There was a wallet with three secret compartments—one for liquids, one for powders, and one for spiders—each carefully designed and unmistakable in its purpose. There was a corkboard with a hundred insects pinned to it—insects that did not exist in nature, did not exist anywhere outside the Emporium.

But that night I was not there for wonders. I was there because I was desperate. And Mr. Handlesropes preys on desperation.

* * *

Mama Alphonz-Custer was the first to play that night. She wanted a map of the city that hung above the fireplace in the secret back room of the Emporium. I had admired that map myself. It showed all the spots where people had fallen in love or seen ghosts. The map sparkled with a million pinprick dots in red and green, all over the city, but with easily discernible concentrations: Branbury Manor, Elsa's Bluffs, Old Forking Street, Portobello Close.

Mr. Handlesropes spent a moment rummaging in his pocket and withdrew a token of leaded glass. He placed it gently on the table, beside his balance. On its surface was a likeness of the map, etched into the glass with exquisite precision.

Mama Alphonz-Custer had nearly ruined herself countless times on such extravagances. I had seen her lose jewelry that had been passed down through her family for generations, magnificent paintings from the collection at Custer Manor, valuable silverware and china, a Stradivarius-Brunel cello. She had also lost the respect of the other Alphonz-Custers, and won it back again. When she wagered too much or too little and lost a family heirloom, they called her a wanton gambler who was squandering the family's fortune and reputation. But when she won, she won such wonders that her family would *ooh* and *aah* in awe, and all would be forgiven: "And to think it didn't cost her a shilling!"

Dame Prudence Weakforce was next. She was a stern woman with a kind heart. She was just as extravagant in her wagers but was never visibly upset when she lost. She treated Mr. Handlesropes's game with an almost scientific disinterest, apparently more concerned with the process itself than with the treasures she stood to win. That night, she told Mr. Handlesropes that she would be playing for the moon chest that stood in the window. Its latches included sensitive gravitational components that kept it locked at all times, save during full moons.

Mr. Handlesropes drew a wheel of cheese from his pocket. Veins of mold patterned its surface, describing the chest in lines of blue green.

Dame Prudence Weakforce smiled as Mr. Handlesropes laid the cheese beside his balance. She had told us once, over drinks at the Crobbleknock, that she suspected Mr. Handlesropes was teasing her, perhaps even flirting with her, through his choice of materials.

The fox-like man was the next to play. He cleared his throat with what sounded like a low growl. He spoke quietly and precisely. "I wish to play for a certain vial in your possession, Mr. Handlesropes. It is a vial on the seventeenth shelf of your third wardrobe. It contains a thick black liquid. A drug, I believe." The man turned to me and met my eyes, and smiled his glittering smile.

My heart stopped. My blood froze and boiled and ceased to circulate. I sweat and shivered and felt hot with sudden fever, with sudden rage. I sat silently, impaled by the fox-man's gaze, as Mr. Handlesropes pulled from his pocket a disk of painted wood depicting the vial in neat brushstrokes. My vial. The vial I needed more than anything in the world.

The fox-man's smile stopped time, so I don't know how long I sat there, transfixed and terrified, but when at last I found myself able to breathe and speak again, Mr. Handlesropes was looking at me expectantly.

I stammered. I babbled. "No, no. He can't. That's mine. It's the thing I want. I need. He can't have it. I need that vial. The one on the seventeenth shelf of your third wardrobe. With the black liquid. I need it. Please." I turned to the man. "Please. You have to . . ."

The man's grin broadened.

Mama Alphonz-Custer and Dame Prudence Weakforce began to whisper to each other. They had never seen two people play for the same item before. None of us knew how that worked. They saw this as an intriguing new development, a bit of vicarious excitement.

I suddenly hated them. "You don't understand," I told them.

Mr. Handlesropes was rummaging again. A look of slight surprise crossed his face, and he shoved both hands into his hip pocket. His old shoulders tensed as he strained at something huge and heavy. His pocket gaped wide—wider than should have been possible—and he heaved something from it that should never have fit in there in the first place.

The table rocked and nearly tipped as Mr. Handlesropes set the thing down with trembling arms. It dwarfed the other tokens, a whale among sardines, a warship among coracles. It was a slab of black iron, cracked and sloppily wrought, a hulking hunk of sheer heaviness with a sketch of the vial scored into its face.

I stared in horror at the massiveness of my need.

The others stared with me. Here was a double wonder—the largest token any of us had ever seen, and definitive proof that the weight of the token varied depending on how much the petitioner valued the object in question. The fox-man's wooden disk sat neat and compact beside my iron monstrosity, each standing in for the same prize. I could see Dame Prudence Weakforce taking shorthand notes in her game diary.

The fox-man smiled to himself with obvious satisfaction. I would have killed him then and there if I thought it would win me the vial, but Mr. Handlesropes did not abide violence in his shop. Behind the curtain, the pianist let out a low growl.

"Well well well well well," said Mr. Handlesropes, who seemed quite amused by the whole thing. "If it isn't an unevenly distributed double entreaty for an irreproducible object of unknown provenance." He gave a little laugh as if he had made a joke. "But we'll cross that bridge if and when we come to it. Mama Alphonz-Custer, your wager, please."

The World of Dew and Other Stories

I watched the proceedings with a peculiar intensity, like a child who finds fascination in anything that is not the horror of an upcoming exam. Mama Alphonz-Custer wagered a tapestry depicting the Alphonz and Custer family trees, with each of the noble clans represented by a different branch, each mythical ancestor by a root. I had seen that tapestry with my own eyes in Custer Museum. It had been kept updated for more than two hundred years, with successive generations adding new branches and sewing creeping chokeweed onto the tree—the weed strangling branches as family members died off or were excommunicated. A recent drought of children meant the chokeweed had nearly reached the highest limbs.

Mr. Handlesropes drew from his pocket a lump of fossilized wood, with an exact copy of that tree chiseled into it. He placed it to the right of the balance.

"Dame Weakforce?"

Dame Prudence Weakforce eyed the cheese, estimating its weight and performing mental algebra. I imagined a set of balances at work in her mind, weighing the cheese against each of her possessions in turn.

"Ariadne, my nightingale," she said at last, "with her cage."

Mr. Handlesropes's hands once again dipped into his pockets. Out came a gorgeous disk of ebony, the bird and cage chalked onto its surface.

Then came the awful man. He licked his lips and paused a moment, but there was no hesitation in that pause. He knew what he was going to wager. "My good Mr. Handlesropes," he said, "I would like to wager the pleasure I take in sneezing."

Mama Alphonz-Custer laughed at this, and Dame Prudence Weakforce jotted furiously in her notebook. They whispered together. "No . . . he can't . . . how?" But Mr. Handlesropes delved into his pockets and withdrew a brass token, much the same size and shape as the one with the vial painted onto it. On its face was a precise depiction of the fox-man's wager—his pleasure in sneezing, eloquent and unmistakable. Mr. Handlesropes placed the token to the right of his balance.

And then it was my turn. I found myself staring at the lump of iron. It filled my vision. I felt its weight on my chest, crushing the breath out

of me. It seemed to heave and pulse, like a living thing, like some grotesque internal organ ripped from a giant.

The others were all staring at me, but they quickly looked away
when I met their gazes. The magnitude of my need was embarrassing
to them. I tried to think like Dame Weakforce, to treat this as a game
and nothing more, an exercise in logic and judgment. All I needed to do
was name something that I valued as much as that little black vial, and
it would be mine at no cost. But what else was so important? What else
did I need so utterly? I found myself unable to think of a single thing
that I owned, as if all my worldly possessions had been repossessed by
the agents of my panic. That iron slab filled my head, blotted out all
else save the vial on the seventeenth shelf of Mr. Handlesropes's third
wardrobe.

The words came without my willing them. For a moment, I thought
they had been spoken by someone else—the fox-man, perhaps. But
then I felt their aftertaste on my lips, I recognized the echo of my own
voice, and I realized that I had indeed spoken the words.

"My son," I had said. "I wager John Magpie, my son."

The whispering and scribbling began again. The fox-man's grin
broadened, and I slumped back miserably in my chair. I had a sense that
Mr. Handlesropes and the others were conspiring against me.

Mr. Handlesropes reached into his pockets, and again he strained
against something big and heavy, something that should not have fit in
any pocket. It was another behemoth, a slab of silver and mother-of-
pearl, with chrome bolts driven through it around its circumference,
and there, in its mirror surface, I saw not my own reflection but my
son's face staring back. I let out a whimper as Mr. Handlesropes heaved
it onto the table opposite the black iron slab.

Mr. Handlesropes snapped his fingers, and the pianist played a
sustained trill, like a circus drumroll, perpetually almost finished, one
step away from resolution.

"The weighing," announced Mr. Handlesropes grandly.

In the left-hand pan of his balance he placed the piece of fossilized
wood that represented Mama Alphonz-Custer's family tapestry; in the
right, the leaded glass. He held the balance steady and then released it
to gravity. It swayed on its fulcrum as the weights fought each other,

then settled at a slant. The fossilized wood was heavier, the tapestry worth more to her. The piano trill resolved to a heavy minor chord—the sound of failure.

Mama Alphonz-Custer let out a hiss of disappointment, and her face turned red. "I knew it," she breathed.

They say you are never really surprised by the outcome of Mr. Handlesropes's game.

Mr. Handlesropes passed the disk of leaded glass to Mama Alphonz-Custer. A reminder of her debt. "I expect delivery of the tapestry by noon tomorrow," he informed her. She nodded sullenly. She would bring it. Nobody ever tried to cheat Mr. Handlesropes.

The piano began its trill again, and Mr. Handlesropes cleared the balance. He placed the wheel of cheese in the left-hand pan; he placed the ebony token in the right-hand pan. When he released the scales, they barely moved at all. The moon-chest cheese and the nightingale ebony weighed the same. Dame Prudence Weakforce smiled to herself. Once again, she had succeeded.

The piano resolved to a triumphant major chord. Mr. Handlesropes gave her the cheese. She would turn it in upstairs, during regular store hours, in exchange for the chest.

Then it was the fox-man's turn. The piano began again. Mr. Handlesropes took the wood and brass tokens in his wrinkled hands and placed them in the pans. As he released the balance, a tremor shot through his old muscles. The balance swayed crazily, and for a moment, I tricked myself into believing they would not balance, but with each sway, the thing shed energy and my hope withered. It reached equilibrium with its arm as straight as the tabletop. The piano sounded a major chord, and Mr. Handlesropes handed over the brass token.

"The vial has been won," announced Mr. Handlesropes. "All further wagers are canceled. I bid you good night, ladies and gentlemen."

I sat numb and shaking. The lump of iron and the glittering silver disk sat on the table, useless and inert. Unweighed. The others packed up their things and headed up the stairs. Dame Prudence Weakforce placed a hand on my shoulder as she passed. A small gesture of compassion. Though I had lost nothing, she seemed to understand the extent of my tragedy. There it was, laid out on the table for all to see.

I was still sitting there when Mr. Handlesropes left the basement. I found myself alone, with my two huge tokens on the table, the balance between them. I reached for them, my hands shaking. A low growl came from behind the curtain, the sound of something straining against chains. I withdrew my trembling hands with a gasp, but I resisted the urge to flee up the stairs. I had to know.

I reached forward again, ignoring the growls, and lifted the two huge tokens onto the scales, not knowing what to hope for.

*　*　*

When I left Mr. Handlesropes's shop, the sun was just beginning to rise. I felt very tired. I had been tired for as long as I could remember, but until now, sleep had been incomprehensible, like a foreign language. Now I felt a tremendous urge to curl up in the doorway of the Emporium and fall asleep on the cold, hard cobbles.

Something moved close by. Someone was waiting for me.

The fox-man spoke in his small, precise voice: "I have something that you want."

"Yes, you do," I said. My exhaustion left me all at once, driven off by sudden adrenaline. I knew the exhaustion would return later, stronger than before, but for now I had all the strength I needed. My fingers tightened around the handle of the knife that I always carried in the seam of my coat.

The fox-man kept his distance, perhaps guessing my intent. He held his hands up to show he did not want trouble.

"What are you?" I hissed. "How did you do it? Why? How did you know about the vial?"

The fox-man smiled his awful smile. "I am a thing of business," he said. "An *entrepreneur*." He made it sound like the name of an animal. "The Fumblers Alley Risk Emporium provides fertile hunting grounds for those such as myself."

Stitches snapped as I pulled my knife from its seam. "Give it to me," I demanded, taking a step toward him.

"A thing that is correctly valued is worth nothing," he continued as if I had not said anything, but he held up his hands again, and this time his posture was threatening, warning me not to come too close.

His fingernails were talons. "You always have to pay full price, and you can never trade it for more than it is worth, so profit is impossible. But when a thing is misvalued—now that's a different matter entirely. Mr. Handlesropes stocks nothing but misvalued goods. His currency is mistakes. He lives on them, trades them on the error markets."

"I did not make a mistake tonight," I told him, raising my knife. "And I would advise you not to make one either. Give me the token."

He pulled the brass disk from his pocket and held it up, taunting me with it. "I live on a different kind of currency," he said. He flashed me his hideous grin, and all at once I realized he was not human.

"How much do you want for it?" I asked, suddenly weak again, my courage fading. "I don't have much money."

"I believe you would give me all the money you possess," the fox-man said. "I believe you would kill for it. I believe you would kill *me*."

"I would," I told him.

"But I am not interested in money. And I am certainly not interested in killing or in being killed over a drug." He snorted. "The vial is worth as much to me as my pleasure in sneezing; it is worth as much to you as your own son. A mutually satisfactory price will therefore fall somewhere in between those two extremes. Clearly you are desperate and willing to resort to violence. I wish to avoid violence, and so this gives you some leverage over me. If I set my price too high, you might judge it worthwhile to risk an attack. This, of course, depends on your judgment of my ability to defend myself. Hmmm. It's all very complicated, isn't it?" He pondered this—or pretended to ponder it. He tapped a fingernail against his teeth, whistled a little tune, mumbled some arithmetic.

Then he named his price.

* * *

My son's brow was very hot. His room stank of sickness. I hadn't noticed the stink before. This was the first time I had spent any length of time outside his room since it had begun, all those weeks ago. I leaned over him and pressed my lips to his burning brow.

"I have it," I whispered, unsure whether he could hear me. "I have the antidote."

His eyelids flickered as I poured the sludgy black liquid down his throat. I winced at the effort it cost him to swallow. He coughed and spluttered, but I made sure he drank it all. Then I gave him some water with sugar and salt. He was too weak to eat, too weak to speak or open his eyes. I could barely remember a time when he had been strong, could barely imagine him running red-cheeked through the playground or climbing the apple tree.

I leaned over him and kissed his forehead again. "You're going to live," I whispered, smiling, my cheeks wet with tears.

Then I did what I had to do. I took my son's laughter from him. He was far too weak to resist. I don't think he even noticed. I took it from him and wrapped it carefully in tissue paper, then in brown packing paper. Then I tied it with string and slipped it into the inside pocket of my coat.

"I had to do it," I repeated to myself, over and over until the words lost their meaning, as I walked back toward Fumblers Alley.

I wondered if he would understand. I wondered if he would forgive me.

The Mugger's Hymn

JOHN GUNN CREPT DOWN FUMBLERS ALLEY ALL JAGGED
nerves and awkward stealth. He hadn't slept a wink in a week. He had
kept himself awake with hits of pirate nicotine and splintery, shivery
adrenaline. He knew that if he slept, he would lose the tune, that better-
than-certainty, that unthinking faith in the world. If he let himself fall
asleep, he would wake up late the next morning hungover, groggy and
miserable, with nothing but fragments of random sound in his head.
Nothing would be worth doing anymore. Who knew how long the depression would last this time?

But for now, drunk on too much wakefulness, it couldn't touch
him. For now, everything was worth it. The line between thought and
action was so thin that it was hardly worth distinguishing anymore.
The little pseudosong pulsed in his ears like a heartbeat.

The streetlights were all burned out in Fumblers Alley. It was a notoriously magical place. They said you could only find it when you were in
the right state of mind—like Narnia, like love—and Gunn understood
that it was destiny that had led him here, now, tonight. He liked the idea
of destiny. It made sense to him. It turned his life into something mean-
ingful. But destiny was like Fumblers Alley—you could only find it and
believe in it at times like this, when the music was playing.

Fumblers Alley was also notoriously dangerous, and Gunn felt
brave and streetwise just by being there. Art addicts and sneaksmiths

hung about in the entrances to the shadowy cellar bars. Muses—men in muscle shirts and tight silk trousers—stared aggressively, daring him to approach, but Gunn ignored them, slipped past like a shadow, as if he were one of them, as if he were used to all this, as if he always came to Fumblers Alley.

All it would take, to make the night catch and sparkle, would be one other person in a similar state of mind, one person who wanted to make a connection, someone else who believed in destiny. It wasn't about sex. It could be anyone, someone with a bright smile and a taste for adventure. Someone who would walk the city streets with him and teach him to see them differently. Someone he might end up kissing or going skinny-dipping with. Or perhaps even singing to.

The mugger was irresistible, did not give Gunn a chance to think. He came at him like gravity. He slammed Gunn against a wall and pinned his arms with big meaty fists, threw shouts at Gunn's face. "Gimme your wallet. Gimme your mothafuckin' wallet." He spoke with a calm, loud anger. There was a terrifying confidence in the way he ordered Gunn to do what he wanted him to do. "Give it to me. Give it to me. Give it to me." Unbearable proximity reduced Gunn's world to the man's sweaty, ugly face. He saw irrational need in the man's eyes.

Afterward, Gunn would imagine all the things he should have done: knees to the crotch, eye gouges, screams that burst the man's eardrums. He would fantasize about superpowers, about turning his body electric, watching the man writhe in pain and drop to the ground, a charred and smoking corpse. About stopping the man's breath with a wave of his hand. He hated the man so much it made him physically sick. If he could have tortured the man to death, he would have.

All he could do—literally all he could do—was reach into his pocket and give the mugger his wallet. It was as if the man took away his free will and was working him like a puppet.

The mugger vanished, lumbering into the darkness with a disdainful lack of hurry, leaving Gunn crumpled on the curb, like an empty bag of chips, stealthy and streetwise no longer. He was on the verge of tears, an overtired little boy. It was in that state that Lucy Much found him.

"Should we give an 'Are you OK?'?" she asked her companion.

"Nah. There's nothing we can do for him."

"I think we should stop. Something's really wrong with him."

"Probably high. A bad trip. Freesound or something. C'mon, we're late."

"No, let's stop."

"Come on, Lucy."

"Oh, fuck off, James. Go on. I'm stopping. No, I mean it. Go."

Then Gunn felt a warm hand on his shoulder. "Are you all right?"

"I think I just got mugged," Gunn blubbered, embarrassed by his words immediately. What did he mean, *I think*?

"Oh fuck, that's terrible. Poor thing. C'mon, you're shivering. On your feet. I'll buy you a hot drink. What do you say? Coffee?"

Fiddlington's on Fumblers served all-night breakfast. Its entrance was dark, like all the entrances to all the establishments on Fumblers Alley, and Gunn would never have dared approach it on his own, but Lucy led him through into the busy, bright interior. They sat in one of the cork-leather booths, and Gunn let the warmth and light and noise of the place slowly repair him. He basked in the wash of conversation and the waitress's bored friendliness.

They drank hickory coffee, and Lucy offered Gunn a nutmeg cigarette. "So what are you doing in Fumblers Alley, anyway?" she asked. "You're not a local. On the prowl for some art? A little bit of music, maybe?"

Gunn considered how he should respond to this. His sleepless confidence was gone, and it was no longer clear to him why he had come to this dangerous part of town. It now seemed stupid and rash. "No. Not art," he said. "Curiosity, I suppose."

Lucy laughed, a little unkindly. "Slumming it."

Gunn wanted to protest, but anything he said would only prove her point, so he just shrugged. "You're local yourself?"

"Transplant from Garricktown, but I've lived here since I was a teenager. So yeah, local, I guess."

"And what do you do?"

"I'm a singer." The word seemed to fall into a silence, as if all the other patrons had paused to draw breath at the same time, two dozen conversations hesitating all at once. Lucy, however, seemed unconcerned.

Gunn glanced around nervously, and Lucy laughed at him again. "Don't worry," she said, "the Enforcers only raid this place on Friday nights. Nobody here cares." She even hummed a little melody out loud, delighting in Gunn's panic. "See?"

"A singer?" Gunn whispered. A shiver of excitement passed through his flesh.

Lucy nodded and sipped her coffee. "Licensed. Officially, I only do little rehab-strength ditties to wean rich addicts off the stuff. But of course I do harder gigs too. You can't live off what Social Services pays."

"A double agent? Like they're always raving about in the papers?"

Lucy grinned. "Yep. Your tax dollars at work training hardened criminals. That's me. Of course they don't train shit. I knew how to sing before the Services hired me. We all do. The suits are all idealism and moral outrage, but the boots on the ground are much more down to earth. You think my reporting officer doesn't know about my gigs?"

"How do you sleep at night?" asked Gunn. Lucy rolled her eyes and motioned for the waitress. "No, no," said Gunn, realizing how it must have sounded. "I don't mean it like that. I mean . . . well . . . I get a song stuck in my head sometimes. I can't sleep. At least I think it's a song."

"Aha," said Lucy. "So the truth comes out. I'm not gonna hook you up, buddy. I *know* you don't have any money."

"No. I'm not an addict. I've never even listened to music, really. I wouldn't recognize it if I heard it. But I get notes stuck in my head sometimes. A part of a song, I think. Or something. I don't know where I got it. Maybe I made it up. It's never more than a few sounds. But they feel like they're going somewhere. You know? Like they have a direction." He was babbling now, but destiny had his tongue. It was too late to stop. "They make me feel like something exciting is about to happen. I can't sleep. I don't want to. Sleep kills it, that little melody. In the morning, it's just a sequence of sounds, all the life gone out of it. So I don't sleep. I walk around the city, waiting for something to happen, seeing where it leads me, because something has to happen. I can feel it. I can hear it coming. That's why I ended up here, in Fumblers Alley. And I think that's why I met you."

Lucy rolled her eyes again. "I'll tell you what happened, honey," she said. "You got fucking mugged. That's what. You ought to go to the police, report your stolen wallet, then go home and go to bed. You'll feel better in the morning."

"No," said Gunn. "I'll feel worse. That would end it. Don't you see? You're where the notes were leading me all along. A song brings me here, to Fumblers Alley, and then I meet you, a singer. We were supposed to meet tonight. Something is supposed to happen between us."

Lucy stared coldly at him, but then she took a sip of coffee, and when she looked up, again her eyes had softened.

"No," she said gently. "That's just how music sounds, honey. Listen to a song a few times, and it tricks you into thinking each note is inevitable. How do you think your mugger felt? But it's just a sham. Life doesn't work that way."

* * *

Gunn had fallen asleep across the plastic table and when he woke up Lucy was gone. She hadn't paid for his coffee, and he found himself stammering and pleading with the waitress, his excuses ringing false, even in his own ears.

The sun was coming up by the time he emerged into Fumblers Alley, leaving promises and apologies at Fiddlington's. The muses, art addicts, and sneaksmiths were all gone, replaced by workers walking briskly in the morning chill with lunch pails in hand. Gunn couldn't tell where the mugging had taken place. The alley was a dull, undifferentiated stretch of gray, in which it was difficult to imagine anything magical or dangerous happening. It was difficult to imagine having met Lucy. The fragment of melody that had brought him to Fumblers Alley was gone from his head.

As he made his way home, hurrying against his own exhaustion, Gunn thought not of Lucy but of the man who had taken his wallet. Perhaps the mugger's head had been full of the inevitability of song as well. Perhaps he had been in the grip of something larger than himself, forced to act against his will, just as he in turn had forced Gunn to give him his wallet.

As he fumbled for his house keys, Gunn came across a business card, loose in his coat pocket: "Lucy Much—Rehabilitation Services." On the back, handwritten in messy pen: "I believe you have a low-level melody dependency—if you're interested in getting better, give me a call."

And there it was, back in his head, that divine inevitability.

The Washerwoman and the Troll

BUNCHUNKLE WAS MAGNIFICENTLY UGLY. THE TROLLMOTHERS said there hadn't been such an ugly child since Grimshik's day, and Bunchunkle wore it with the pride and mirth befitting a troll. He could pull a face to make you void your bowels and howl with terror. He had a genius for mischief that rivaled even that of old Quillibim, the Arch Rascal of Moldy Stumps. There was much speculation about what would happen if a human ever laid eyes on Bunchunkle, but as far as anyone knew, it had never happened, for Bunchunkle was as quick and sly as he was ugly.

When the faefolk decided it was time to drive the old washerwoman from the Blinking Woods, they did not come to Bunchunkle immediately. He was reclusive and cantankerous and did not like to be disturbed. Besides, they were loath to seek him out for fear of laying eyes on his revolting face. But nobody doubted that he would succeed if all else failed. They knew he was there as a last resort.

The washerwoman had arrived earlier that autumn and had built a shack down by the river from mud and reeds. She was a sorry sight, stooped and half-blind. Her hands were cracked and dry from the harsh soaps she used in her work, and she bent double beneath the weight of the wicker washbaskets that she bore upon her back. Her long pointed chin nearly touched the ground as she labored to and from Hintershed Village, carrying those baskets like a snail carries her shell.

"She's not long for this world," hissed Queen Calahadria gleefully. She delighted in the aging of mortals, finding immense humor in the inescapability of their deaths. She couldn't help but laugh to think of it. It was like knowing there was a hilarious punch line coming at the end of an otherwise rambling and pointless story.

"Don't be so sure," cautioned Grognorp of the Puffballs. "She has that boy-child of hers to care for. You mark my words—she'll not let herself die until he's old enough to survive on his own, and that might be some time. I don't recall just how long it takes for a human boy to mature, but it's too damn long, if you ask me."

Although Grognorp was a cynic and a bore, there was general agreement among the faefolk that his assessment of the situation was correct and that having a mortal living in their domain was becoming tiresome. So at the next Grand Bonfire, plans for mischief were laid.

* * *

First, Blistermuck, the shellycoat, hid in the river, and when the washerwoman began to soap a load of laundry in the rocky shallows, he snatched the edge of a bedsheet and dragged it down to the muddy bottom. The old woman cried out and splashed into the water after the sheet, scared and unsteady in the strong current. But it was too late. She could only watch the white sheet disappear into the murky depths, as if of its own accord. She never saw the shellycoat, but she heard a sound like wet laughter blopping up to the surface.

From that day on, every time the washerwoman brought a load of laundry to the river's edge, Blistermuck would steal any garments he could get his muddy hands on. Sometimes it was socks, sometimes underthings or a pillowcase, and once it was her washboard and soap. The washerwoman wept with rage and frustration, but she kept coming back, day after day, with her basket full of laundry, for this was her livelihood, and she and the child both depended on it.

And she did not leave the Blinking Woods.

Next, Blattersworth and Ogretta, the hobgoblins, took up residence in her hut and filled it with dangerous inconveniences. They charmed up roots from the ground to catch her feet as she went about her endless chores; they whispered to the coals in her fireplace so that they would not catch; they hid desperately needed tools and spread mold on her food; they spent the night under her bed, and each time she was about to fall asleep, they tickled her nose with a stalk of wild mustard, causing her to wake, spluttering and sneezing.

And although the washerwoman tripped and fell again and again, until she had shattered every dish in the house and her hands and knees were blue with bruises; although she tried for hours to light her fire and went to bed crying and shivering, wrapping herself around the child to keep him warm; although she spent entire evenings searching for her needle and thread, or her soup ladle, or her tinderbox; although she had to scrape a layer of mold off every piece of food she ate; although she wept and screamed and stood in silent disbelief at her misfortune, still she remained, with the young boy, who was her ward.

Still she did not leave the Blinking Woods.

Then, one day, the Birchling sisters stole the child away. They revealed themselves to the boy while the washerwoman foraged for mushrooms, and they led him into the secret depths of the forest. He followed with hands outstretched, his belly brimming with laughter, trying to catch the nimble little faeries in his fat fingers. The sisters flitted through the branches on gossamer wings. They were radiant in the darkness, and they cackled and whispered in the boy's ear, promising that he would have games and magic and desserts if he would only come a little farther. He followed them all night, and all the next day, going deeper and deeper into the woods, until the branches were so thick overhead that even the strongest sunshine could not reach there, and still he followed the laughter and dance of the Birchling sisters. He followed them for a week, and then a year, and then a hundred years more. He followed them until he grew old and wrinkled, and still he followed with his arms outstretched and laughter in his belly. He followed until he was old and stooped like his grandmother, the washerwoman. And then one day he could follow no more, and the Birchling sisters left him in the woods and returned to their pine-cone home having only been gone a moment, for such was the magic of brownies.

But still the washerwoman did not leave the Blinking Woods.

She no longer had any washing to do. Her reputation for losing garments, or bringing them back stained with river mud, had ruined her career. She never went into Hintershed Village anymore, and the villagers shrugged and let their clothes grow dirty. The washerwoman spent each day searching for her grandson, calling his name and venturing deeper and deeper into the secret depths of the forest, disturbing the faefolk all the more. She lived off whatever mushrooms and berries and seeds she found during her wandering, and although Umpa, the imp, made a sport of swapping her edible mushrooms for poisonous ones, and although she often grew terribly ill, she did not die, and neither did she leave the Blinking Woods. She just kept on stumbling through the forest's forgotten darknesses, calling the child's name.

* * *

"It's no good," grumbled Grognorp at the next Grand Bonfire. "She's as stubborn as a natterjack toad. And now she's more determined than ever to stay. Mark my words—she won't give up on the boy now."

"Then let's give him back to her," giggled Marrowtree, the dryad.

So they fashioned a changeling from bundles of rushes held together with beeswax, and Winderwinks, the April elf, glamoured it up with a likeness of the boy.

When the washerwoman found the changeling child, a month after the Birchling sisters had stolen away her true grandson, she did not speak. She just gathered the bundle of rushes and wax up in her arms, brought it home, and laid it down in the boy's cot. Then she went down to the river and wept in the moonlight.

"She knows something is amiss," hissed Tagglehop from where he hid among the brambles.

"She fears for her sanity," whispered Skambles, the briar goblin.

The changeling child did not speak. Neither did it laugh nor cry nor sleep. It just lay in its cot and gurgled and stared. And yet whenever the washerwoman fed it, or changed its clothes, or bathed it, she thought she could hear laughter filling her hut—a cruel and mocking laughter.

But still the washerwoman did not leave the Blinking Woods.

She tended to the changeling in silence and with great patience. She did not play with the child anymore. Neither did she speak to it, nor sing the old lullabies that she used to sing. She took care of it with a chilly detachment, as if she did not trust it. Or perhaps she did not trust herself anymore. Something like resentment appeared in her feeble eyes, and sometimes when she went down to the river's edge at night, she would scream at the moon, like a wolf.

* * *

That was when Grognorp went to fetch Bunchunkle.

As he approached the bone-strewn threshold of the troll's toadstool home, Grognorp tied a heavy blindfold around his eyes to spare himself the sight of Bunchunkle's hideous face.

"Troll! You're needed!" he shouted. "We've tried everything. She just stays, despite her fear and unhappiness. She stays and stays. Calahadria says it's *because* of her fear and unhappiness that she stays, but I can't fathom that. Anyway, we need you, you heap of rotten mutton. We need your ugliness. We want you to show yourself to her. No mortal could stand the look of you, you filthy piece of beetle dung. The shock of it'll surely drive her mad, maybe kill her, or worse."

There was no answer at first, and Grognorp stood sheepishly in front of Bunchunkle's door, wondering if the troll was deliberately ignoring him or if he had gone abroad in the forest without anyone noticing.

"Bunchunkle?" he shouted again. "Bunchunkle!"

Feeling like a fool, Grognorp took off his blindfold with the intention of asking the nearby trees if they knew the young troll's whereabouts. But as soon as his eyes were uncovered, there was Bunchunkle, nose to nose with him, laughing a nasty, spittle-flecked laugh, right in his face. Grognorp stumbled backward in shock and revulsion, tripped over a bat's skull, and fell flat on his back. This only made Bunchunkle laugh more, and the very sound of it made Grognorp nauseous. He shut his eyes tight and repeated his plea. "Bunchunkle, we need you. Scare her out of our woods."

"Bunchunkle never showed his face for no mortal afore," said the troll once he had stopped laughing. His voice was like roots and old rot. "Wherefore he do it? What says the Bonfire Folk?"

Grognorp got to his feet and forced himself to look the troll in his bulging red eyes. "The boy's bones," he said. "If you succeed, you can have them."

"Oh-ho," said Bunchunkle, dancing a clumsy troll jig. "Them's a fine morsel. The Birchling sisters show Bunchunkle when and where they are?"

"Yes. Where and when," said Grognorp. "But only if the washerwoman leaves the Blinking Woods and does not come back."

"Fret not," Bunchunkle assured him. "Such irresistible ugliness as mine will surely drive her mad and from the woods both."

*   *   *

That night, for the first time in many moons, the coals caught in the washerwoman's hearth, and she had light and warmth in her crumbling hut. A glimmer of a smile crossed her lips as she hung a kettle of water above the fire and set some wild potatoes and sprigs of rosemary to bake among the coals. When the water was hot, she stripped the changeling child of its clothes and lifted it into her wooden washtub.

She still had a small fragment of the soap she had once used to wash her laundry. As she poured the steaming water over the child, she rubbed its skin with the fragrant fragment and sang over it, as she had not done since she brought the changeling home. But as she bathed the child, the hot water began to melt the wax that held the bundles of rushes together, and the changeling came apart before her eyes. As it disintegrated, the glamour faded, and soon there was nothing in her tub but rushes and blobs of wax, floating on the surface of the warm water.

The washerwoman let out a small and pitiful moan. She raised her trembling hands before her face and stared at them, as if they had been responsible for the transformation, and then she slumped to the ground, hugging her knees to her chest.

That was when Bunchunkle began to laugh. In the past, the laughter of the faefolk had always come as a distant, ethereal sound, only half heard. But Bunchunkle's laughter was solid and earthy, full of filth and fire, and the washerwoman heard it clearly, echoing about her hut like a trapped moth. She got to her feet, shakily, and turned to see Bunchunkle standing on the stump that she used as a chopping block, tiny and naked and scowling—a toadstool troll, the ugliest since Grimshik, laughing at her in her own hut.

The washerwoman stared for a long time in dumbfounded silence while Bunchunkle pulled grotesque faces. He had made daemons scream in terror with such faces. He had caused trees to uproot themselves and flee from him. He had turned owls blind and made foxes lose their appetites. But the washerwoman did not scream or flee or go blind. She did not even look away. She just stared at the little troll standing on her chopping block. And then she did something that nobody had ever done to Bunchunkle before: she laughed at him.

It began as a spluttering giggle that might have been a sob, but as it grew, it became a full-blown bout of breathless, belly-shaking laughter. She laughed loud and hard, drowning out Bunchunkle's own trollish cackles. She laughed until tears streamed from her eyes and she wet herself, and then she stripped off her soiled clothes, lifted the washtub in her shaking arms, and poured the hot water over her head. When she noticed the blobs of wax and waterlogged rushes tangled in her wiry gray hair, she laughed all the more.

When at last the washerwoman regained her composure, Bunchunkle was staring at her. The little troll blushed and scowled, feeling a curious mixture of anger, embarrassment, and fascination. This washerwoman—this *mortal*—had not vomited in terror. She had not dropped dead or turned to stone. She had laughed at him. And now she was standing stark naked, dripping with bathwater, and smiling down at him as if his legendary ugliness were nothing but a joke.

"Oh, little troll," she said to him. "You and your kin have tormented me for too long. I feared you once, but now I am beyond fear. I hated you once, but now I am beyond hate. I thought that you were evil, but now I understand that you are neither good nor evil, as a storm is neither good nor evil, as a mushroom is neither good nor evil. Happiness and misery mean nothing to you. I see all this in your face, for it is not a face wrought by God, but by some vast, uncaring power."

The washerwoman leaned in close and studied Bunchunkle intently. When she spoke again, Bunchunkle could smell mortality on her breath: "I will learn to become like you," she said. "I am tired of good and evil, of happiness and misery. I have had more than enough for one lifetime. I will become like a storm, like a mushroom."

And as easily as she had shed her clothes, the washerwoman shed her mortality. She left it there on the ground, in a puddle of bathwater, and she skipped out into the Blinking Woods, naked and laughing, to join the faefolk in their games and mischief.

But poor, hideous Bunchunkle stood on the chopping block in a state of sheer confusion, scratching his bald head with a corkscrew thumbnail. He felt uncertain about who he was, baffled and adrift from himself. For the first time in his life, his ugliness had failed him, and a troll without his ugliness is like a bird without her wings, or an elf without her magic. A troll without his ugliness is just a tiny ferocious human.

"Hmph," he growled to himself, looking around the little mud hut. "No, Bunchunkle couldn't. Well, then again, perhaps he could. Perhaps he could indeed."

* * *

Bunchunkle failed to drive the washerwoman from the Blinking Woods, and so he did not receive his reward. The boy's bones were not found and will not be found for another hundred years. But the people of Hintershed Village say that sometimes, if you listen closely, you can hear the sound of laughter and running feet coming from the haunted depths of the woods.

The villagers say other things as well.

They say that if you leave your laundry in the bole of a certain hollow tree at the edge of the Blinking Woods, it will come back the next day as clean and bright and fresh as a spring morning.

They also say that if you are foolish enough to venture into the Blinking Woods at night, and if you are lucky enough to go during the right phase of the moon, and if you are powerful enough to shake the glamour from your eyes, and if you are clever enough to avoid getting lost among the shifting trees and the trap paths, and if you manage to break through all the wards that protect the Grand Bonfire from outsiders and you happen to stumble upon it, you might see an old woman with rushes in her hair, skyclad and wild-eyed, dancing and laughing amid an unspeakable gathering of faefolk, with whom no mortal should consort.

And if you happen to continue on a little way, to the edge of the river, you might see a hideous troll, with a woman's mortality draped around his small shoulders like a shawl, whistling happily to himself as he attends to baskets brimming with dirty laundry.

Professor Jennifer Magda-Chichester's Time Machine

PROFESSOR JENNIFER MAGDA-CHICHESTER STOOD ON THE stage of Stockholm Concert Hall, smiling proudly into a sea of tuxedos. "It is a great honor to receive this most prestigious of awards," she said, a cluster of ubiquitous nanomicrophones reproducing her every word in perfect fidelity in the minds of a million listeners worldwide. "A very great honor. The greatest that any scientist can ever hope to achieve. I am very proud of my team, and of course I am indebted to all the brilliant minds who laid the foundation for my work. If I have seen farther than others, it is because I have stood on the shoulders of giants.

"And yet my near-perfect happiness on this day is tainted by the tiniest speck of regret. I am an old woman, and as you all know by now, the device can only travel *backward* through time. I therefore stand here before you today in the full knowledge that I will never live to see my invention reach its full potential. I can only imagine all the wonderful uses that future generations will find for the thing. Did Alan Turing imagine all the benefits of today's sentient quantum computers? Did Neil Armstrong imagine the wonders of Luna Colony Alpha?"

The professor paused for a moment, letting her audience consider the potential of backward time travel, letting them consider how limited their own imaginations were, letting them imagine how much they couldn't imagine. She had always believed that the most important quality in a scientist was an awareness of how much was beyond one's understanding.

Then she delivered her punch line, gesturing to the machine with a grin. "Well, I guess we'll just have to go back and ask them."

* * *

And yet it didn't happen like that. It happened nearly a decade earlier, and someone entirely different had stood on that stage in Stockholm, graciously accepting the prize, dispensing words of wisdom and bon mots to the enraptured crowd. Jennifer Magda-Chichester had wasted the last ten years of her career working stubbornly on an invention that her onetime mentor Professor Maxwell Honksworthy had invented and patented years earlier. She had simply refused to believe that he had gotten there first. The Nobel Prize was nothing but a fantasy, born of envy and denial.

"You bastard," she breathed, the taste of lutefisk still fresh in her mouth, despite never having existed. "Two can play at that game."

* * *

Professor Jennifer Magda-Chichester invented her time machine in the late '90s. The announcement came out of the blue. Nobody within the scientific community saw it coming. It was that rarest of things— an invention that seemed beholden to nothing that had come before it, born sui generis from the mind of a solitary genius. When, during her Nobel Prize acceptance speech, Professor Jennifer Magda-Chichester made the obligatory reference to standing on the shoulders of giants, the audience actually jeered. Her work was so original and groundbreaking that they wouldn't accept any false modesty.

* * *

Except that that was nonsense. It was basically the same invention for which the prize had been awarded to Professor Maxwell Honksworthy in the mid-'80s.

* * *

One of the most curious technological innovations to come out of the Second World War was Jennifer Magda-Chichester's time machine, developed in secret at Bletchley Park but allegedly never used until after the war was over. Although much admired for her brilliant mind, the device's eccentric inventor received harsh criticism for her refusal to use the machine to go back in time and assassinate Hitler.

*　*　*

Maxwell Honksworthy was the enigmatic figure at the center of one of history's most controversial criminal trials. His case provides us with a thorny ethical dilemma. Does his world-changing invention, and the knowledge he claims to have gained from its use, justify his murder of the innocent child Adolf Hitler?

*　*　*

Professor Magda-Chichester was without doubt the most creative and influential figure to emerge from the bohemian movement in fin de siècle Europe. Her feminist ideas were decades, if not centuries, ahead of their time, but she made her greatest contributions in the field of science. Working alone in a remote laboratory in West Sussex, she invented and built the world's first working time machine, a staggering achievement that required her to invent entire scientific disciplines essentially from scratch. H. G. Wells is said to have given up writing upon meeting her, saying, "Jennifer makes my fiction irrelevant."

Quite apart from its practical uses, the time machine forever laid to rest claims of female intellectual inferiority, thus validating Professor Magda-Chichester's arguments in favor of equal rights for women.

*　*　*

Lord Maxwell Honksworthy made his fortune as an inventor and industrialist. His corporation, the Royal Honksworthy Company, produced many of the nineteenth century's most profitable inventions, including the light bulb, pasteurization (a process he mockingly named after a French chemist who had been pursuing a similar line of research at the time), and the robotic butler. His greatest invention, however, is the Honksworthy Time Machine.

* * *

The writings of Lady Magda-Chichester give some insight into the life of one of the most brilliant and enigmatic figures of Renaissance England. She was given a peerage by Queen Elizabeth for her invention of what was then known as Her Majesty's Chronic Engine—the device on which all modern time machines are based. Little is known about Magda-Chichester prior to her peerage, but her diaries and personal correspondence give a picture of a woman at odds with the mores of her time. She was deeply troubled by the low status accorded to women and minorities in Elizabethan England, even though it was one of the most progressive societies in the world at that time; furthermore, she seemed revolted by prevailing standards of hygiene and sanitation.

Although she writes of her great pleasure in witnessing Shakespeare's plays and listening to the music of William Byrd, it seems she led a deeply unhappy life. The final entry in her diary, dated 1625, simply reads, "I went too far."

* * *

An intriguing fragment of manuscript has recently been unearthed in a crypt beneath the ruined monastery of Kilfarlich. The manuscript seems to describe a machine that was capable of traveling backward through time, created by a magician. Sadly, the manuscript is incomplete. If such a precursor to Lady Magda-Chichester's famous device ever existed, the identity of its inventor and the specifics of its workings are lost to history.

Joey LeRath's Rocket Ship

BILLY MET JOEY LERATH THE SAME DAY HE LOST HIS FAMILY in Crouchtree Market. His parents had gotten into one of their rows over at the nuclear-weapons stand, and his little sister had started to cry, so Billy had run off, not really paying attention to where he was going. He hated hearing his parents fight and his little sister cry. These last few days he had heard little else, and he was sick of it. So he ran until they were drowned in the market hubbub, and he never found them again.

Billy ran past stalls selling fishing rope and spiced nuts and sundries and secrets; he ran through crowds of men in top hats, thickets of women with parasols and prams, gaggles of grimy children playing conkers and booboo and shake 'em; he ran until he was tired, and when he finally stopped running, he realized he was thoroughly lost.

Just as Billy was starting to wonder if he should be scared, there was Joey LeRath in his filthy duffle coat, holding a piece of caramel wrapped in wax paper between his corkscrew fingernails.

"Hey, kid," Joey said, his voice like unoiled gears grinding together. "Want some candy?"

Joey smelled like smoke and oil and sweat, and his face was smeared with engine grease. He hadn't bathed in at least a year. He was skinny and twisted, and his duffle coat clung tight and awkward to his frame, as if it were holding on for dear life. On his head, he wore a tattered beret that was held together with safety pins and bits of string. He had a wild look in his eyes, one of which was much bigger than the other.

"C'mere," he said. "I've got something amazing to show you. Something you ain't never seen before."

Billy liked the look of Joey, so he took the candy, ate it, and followed the old man into Crumblefoot Alley, to the trash pile behind the crematorium.

Joey had fashioned his rocket ship from cardboard and tin, with soup-can radar and portholes made from the doors of salvaged tumble dryers. It stood at the center of a crater of charred trash, like a fat, battered dart that had been dropped onto a blackened bull's-eye and then flipped onto its flights to point triumphantly, or rudely, at the sky.

The rocket ship was powered by a deuterium-tritium hybrid inertial confinement fusion reactor, which Joey had built from scratch. The reactor was housed in a rusty old steamer trunk, bolted to the body of the ship, its latches long since broken, its lid askew. Clouds of steam billowed from its innards.

"C'mon on in, kid. I'll show you round," said Joey. Billy followed him up the fraying rope ladder, and they crawled into the cramped cockpit. Inside, it smelled of rust and mildew, and Joey had to bend double to avoid bumping his head. Somehow he looked more comfortable, hunched and crooked like that, as if his very bones were twisted.

"This is just a prototype," Joey explained. "One day I'll build a full-size one and fly into space myself, exceptin' if I die first, heh. This one's built to one-third scale. That's why I need a kid your size to test her out. See if she works right."

Joey sized up Billy with his mismatched eyes, then clapped him on the shoulder, too hard. "You look like a plucky kid. Yeah, you'll do all right. Oh, I ain't saying it ain't dangerous. This baby's dangerous as hell. But you look like one hell of a pilot. You'll get her into space or die trying, am I right? What didja say your name was?"

"Didn't," said Billy. He told Joey his name, and Joey told Billy his in return. They shook hands, like grown-ups did.

"Anyway," said Billy, "it was nice meeting you, sir, but I should really go and find my parents now."

Joey shook his head sadly. "Oh, Billy-me-boy," he said, "I'm afraid not. You lost your parents in Crouchtree Market. And when you lose something in Crouchtree Market, you never find it again."

Billy looked at Joey wide-eyed, full of sudden panic. "My parents? My little sister? No, I don't believe you." He scrambled out the hatch and down the rope ladder, clambered over the rim of the trash crater, and dashed to the mouth of Crumblefoot Alley.

Billy emerged into unfamiliar streets. The neighborhood was filling with afternoon shadow, emptying of people. There was no sign of Crouchtree Market or of his family. Everyone had gone.

Joey LeRath appeared by Billy's side and put one bony hand on the boy's shoulder. "That's what Crouchtree Market is like," he said sadly. "She's a restless old market. Never stays in one place for long. Not a place to bring children. I hate to say it, Billy-me-boy, but it looks to me like your parents lost you accidentally-on-purpose."

Sobs grabbed for Billy's throat, heaved themselves up and out of him. "No," he managed, spluttering teary outrage. "It was *me* who ran away from *them*!"

But a horrible uncertainty rose in Billy like puke. Just the night before, he had overheard too-loud whispers coming from his parents' bedroom—angry accusations, whispers that wanted to be screams, whispers he wished he could unhear: "You want to tear this family apart. . . . You would do this to our children? . . . You don't love us anymore?"

"They . . ." started Billy, but he was crying hard now, and the words came out as ragged gulps. "I'll never see . . . them again? Mum, Dad . . . little sister?"

"I'm afraid not, Billy," said Joey gently. He stood for a moment in silence with his hand on Billy's shoulder as snot and tears dripped from the boy's face. But then Joey crouched close to Billy and grinned. "Bah. Forget about them," he said. "Where you're going, you don't need families. The sun and the moon'll be your parents. Shooting stars will be your little sisters. Space is waiting for you, Billy. The countdown has already begun."

* * *

Joey tied Billy into the captain's chair with lengths of fraying rope—"for safety." He showed him the gear shifter, the steering wheel, and the ejector seat. He explained the basics of six-axis maneuvering and orbital dynamics. He made Billy a pot of tea and set it beside the captain's chair—"for emergencies." Then he began the countdown. "Ten. Nine." Joey crawled out the hatch and locked it behind him. "Eight," he said, his voice tinny and muffled.

Blastoff came at "seven" and was sudden enough that Billy had no time to get scared. The ship bucked and shook as fire belched from its rocket engines. The heat and noise were so intense that Billy's eyes wouldn't work, but he felt in his bones that the ground was all-of-a-sudden very far below him, and was getting very-farther with every passing all-of-a-sudden. The crush of acceleration held Billy to his seat, like a bully, and this feeling of terrible heaviness seemed in direct contradiction with his sensation of being borne upward at tremendous speed, yet Billy knew the two feelings were really one.

The rocket ship was fast and loud and on fire. That was all Billy could really tell from his seat. It punched through the earth's atmosphere like a nail through cotton, like a gunshot through a dream. It roared and blazed and quaked, an explosion that wouldn't stop exploding. And then, with shocking abruptness, it did stop. Everything stopped at once.

A weightless silence flooded the ship. Billy realized he was holding his breath, and he couldn't remember how long he had been holding it for, so he let it out and sucked in a big fresh lungful, just to be sure. The air tasted metallic and recycled, but it seemed to relax Billy and clear the fuzz from his brain, so he breathed some more of it. Then he poured himself some tea from the pot that sat by his elbow and gulped it down, grateful for its bitter warmth.

Billy untied himself from the captain's chair and rose into the air. The cramped conical cockpit seemed newly voluminous with this third dimension to play in. Billy spun lazily counterclockwise as he rose, powerless to do otherwise, until he bumped gently against the burlap-and-egg-carton wall. A set of bicycle handlebars jutted from the bulkhead by his shoulder, perfect for grabbing, so Billy levered himself upside down and kicked off again. He spiraled and somersaulted around the ship; he tumbled and drifted and flew. He whooped. He took off a shoe and threw it. It flipped and bounced about without any indication that it would ever slow down or come to a rest. He tried to pour himself some more tea but found it billowed from the pot's spout in a wobbling blob instead of arcing into the cup like it ought to have done. While he was engrossed in the shapes that the tea made, his shoe took an unlucky bounce and kicked him in the back of the head. He laughed at the ridiculousness of it.

"Space," he said out loud. "I'm in space."

Then he looked down on the majesty of the earth.

It was an unthinkable vastness of blue and green and brown, strewn with cloud, sunlight, shadow. And yet it was somehow a single object. It filled all the portholes. Gray smears of cities were visible, and plumes of dark smoke from forest fires, strings of white-headed mountains, deserts in yellows and reds and browns. And far off to starboard, Billy could see the terminator line, the battlefront of night, devouring color as it advanced, spoiling the earth's too-perfect geometry.

Billy hadn't considered what he would do once he got to space, and he wasn't sure Joey LeRath had either, but he was happy to be there. He liked the cool solitude of orbit, the weightless freedom, the far-awayness of it all.

The flood of adrenaline that the launch had released began to drain out of Billy, and all at once he felt very tired, so he curled up in midair and went to sleep, spinning very slowly end over end.

Far below him, the sparkle of detonating warheads, the blooming of mushroom clouds.

The Visible Spectrum

I HAD JUST LEFT MY JOB AT THE CNIB TO WORK WITH THE UN FULL-time when they discovered it. We had less than forty years to prepare.

We began with agriculture. We built huge vertical farms, fifty-story skyscrapers in which most of the work could be automated. They were in the pipeline anyway, they used land so efficiently. Traditional farming would still continue, of course. I met an old man in Alberta who claimed he could plow his fields blindfolded. He became our first spokesman. We built sensors for tractors, installed guide wires along the edges of fields, developed a range of cheap equipment to identify common pests and diseases.

Transportation actually improved. We installed extensive street-car networks in all major cities, strung ropes along the edges of side-walks. We consolidated populations, drawing suburbanites back downtown. We ripped up highways and laid rail. Trains have been able to drive themselves for decades, held back only by union pressure and a public mistrust of automation.

A few pundits claimed the whole thing was a conspiracy to push an environmentalist agenda. But for once fear was on our side. People trusted us because they were scared not to. I was scared too, maybe more than anyone.

When I first became chair of the UN Accessibility Committee, it was a largely ceremonial position. After the announcement, though, I was the most important person in the world. I was young and smart and ambitious, and I took charge when someone needed to. I got the Canadian government on board right away; I had old school friends in Parliament. Australia and the UK joined in shortly after. When other countries saw how quick we were moving, they were scared to be left behind. Before long, we had a blank check and an army of staff. I met with world leaders daily, me and Bess. I swear that dog met more heads of state than most heads of state do. It was terrifying.

This was all before I met your grandfather.

Taxes went way up everywhere, of course, but there was also an economic boom. There was just so much work to be done. Everyone compared it to a wartime economy.

We manufactured two hundred thousand Perkins Braillers in that first year and ramped up production from there. Google had already digitized most of the world's books, so once we had the infrastructure set up, it was easy to start producing Braille editions. All new laptops came with refreshable Braille displays as well as regular screens. They came with built-in software designed to gradually wean users off visual feedback and get them hooked on the RBDs. We called them *transitional technologies*. For decades, TT was an important marketing symbol.

Ironically, I spent a lot of time on TV during those years, demonstrating new technologies and showing viewers what life would be like after it happened.

* * *

A close-up of my face: "Instead of watching sports on TV, we'll just have to get up off our couches and start actually playing!"

Zoom out to reveal me in sweatpants and T-shirt standing on a goalball court. I block the jingling ball with my hand, judging its position by sound alone.

* * *

Your grandfather saw me on TV before we ever met. He said he knew right away. Imagine that! Falling in love with someone based on what they look like. It was ridiculous. But ridiculous did it for me at that time. Everyone was taking everything so seriously that sometimes being ridiculous was the only way to cope.

The blind—those who were blind already—set themselves up as consultants and charged exorbitant fees. There were several cases of fraud, of sighted people trying to cash in by pretending to be blind, with dogs and canes for disguises. Conspiracy theorists even claimed that the blind were behind it all, fed up with not having the world tailored to meet our needs. As I was the public face of all these changes, they often targeted me specifically. I just ignored them.

There were religious fanatics, of course, who claimed it was divine judgment on the world, the ninth plague of Egypt all over again, the beginning of the End Times. I sometimes had to address these claims in my media appearances, always treating them as jokes, turning them to our advantage. "I hardly think this is a plague worthy of God. It might have been nasty for the ancient Egyptians, but with today's technology, it is little more than a minor inconvenience."

Shortly after he and I started dating, your grandfather dropped by my house late in the evening. He said he was taking me on a picnic. I told him I had already eaten, but he insisted. He drove us out to the beach in his little hatchback and spread a blanket on the sand. We listened to the noisy surf and ate a baguette with brie, drank some wine. It was all very romantic, but when I touched his face, I realized he was crying.

"It's the stars," he told me. Have you learned about stars yet, in school? Anyway, he was an amateur astronomer, your grandfather. With sight, you could do astronomy with cheap equipment, or even with no equipment at all.

"The stars," he said with a quiver in his voice. "Where would we be if we couldn't look up and see the stars? We wouldn't have navigation or the constellations or *Star Trek*." Yes, of course we had *Star Trek*. This was back before the radio show though. It was on television back then.

I think I laughed at him, which might have been cruel, but it was a habit by that point. It was my job to make this stuff seem like no big deal. Besides, it seemed like a funny thing to cry about.

"We have GPS," I pointed out, kissing away his tears. "We can navigate just fine. And as for the constellations and *Star Trek*—they're imaginary! There will never be a shortage of imagination."

Then I told him about a calculus problem I was assigned in university. I had to calculate the rate of change of a man's shadow as he walked past a streetlight. My professor had found a way of explaining it to me. "Imagine a gnome sitting on top of the lamppost holding a long extendable stick. He likes to rest the far end of the stick on the heads of passersby on the street below, but it always extends all the way to the ground. The distance from the passerby's feet to the end of the stick is the length of his shadow."

"Gnomes," said your granddad. And then he smiled.

You'll have to ask your grandfather to tell you what it was like to see. From what I could gather, everybody thought of it as direct, unmediated experience of reality. Of course it was really just photons bouncing around—but there was a precision to it that was awfully impressive. With sight, you could easily jump from rock to rock in a river without getting your feet wet. I guess it was like having proximity sensors built right into your brain.

* * *

Close-up on my face, lit by a flashlight: "They say destiny is written in the stars." Pan up to reveal a brilliantly starry sky tinged with the green of the aurora borealis. I am in Nunavut. "And, indeed, astronomers were among the first to notice the impending change."

Cut to an astronomer sitting in front of an impressive telescope. "So will you be out of a job once it happens?"

The astronomer laughs. "Lord no! We astronomers are used to dealing with things we can't see. I can't remember the last time I looked through an optical telescope. Our equipment measures a huge spectrum of radiation, of which visible light is only a tiny portion. It will just be a matter of displaying the data differently."

Cut to an amusing clip from *Futurama* of Professor Farnsworth using his smelloscope.

* * *

People flocked to see visual art in those days, knowing it was their last chance. Critics wrote about the frantic atmosphere in galleries, the sense of anxiety and desperation with which visitors stared at the paintings and sculptures. Actual sales of visual art plummeted, of course, and artists—ever adaptable—began to experiment with sound, touch, smell, and taste in new and exciting ways. Even before it happened, galleries began putting on exhibits designed to be experienced in the dark. Many prominent artists are on record saying it was the best thing that ever happened to the art world.

Emergency services took a lot of work. We decentralized firefighting, went back to small-scale volunteer departments. Firefighters memorized the layouts of the units they were responsible for.

*   *   *

"It's often impossible to see in a smoky building, anyway," I tell the camera as beefy firefighters practice lifts and drags behind me. "In the most dangerous situations, firefighters may well be as effective as ever. And with new regulations regarding heating, appliances, and sprinkler systems, we actually expect deaths from fire to go down."

A blindfolded firefighter in bunker gear lifts me over his shoulder and carries me out of shot.

Cut to a shot of me sitting on an examining table. I am surrounded by an array of medical gizmos. "Many pieces of diagnostic equipment will function as they always have," I say, sticking a stethoscope into my ears. Audio of a heart thumping. "Blood-pressure tests, urine and fecal tests, electrocardiograms—even x-rays and MRIs—will all continue to function in pretty much the same way, just with auditory or tactile output. Diagnosis of things like rashes will get more difficult, but internal medicine will remain almost identical."

*   *   *

Your mother was born about thirty years before it happened. I think it was considerably easier for her generation than for mine. She was born knowing that vision would not last. It was like getting her first period or her driver's license, something that was just a part of growing up. The TT concept had been applied to the whole of society by then. Kids attended school blindfolded, and they could all function effectively both blind and sighted. It was like your French immersion program. We called them *ambi-abled*, and the adults envied them. Those of my generation were too set in their ways, too slow to learn new things. That's why old people grumble so much.

If there was one event that really changed people's attitudes, it was the first blind flight. The pilot flew from London to St. John's blindfolded, using tactile feedback, and he nailed the landing in high crosswinds. It was a cheesy publicity stunt and a little disingenuous at that, because the really hard part of aviation was air traffic control. But that pilot captured the world's imagination. He was made an honorary colonel in the RCAF, became a household name. After that, people really started to believe that everything was going to be all right.

We picked a day. It didn't happen like that, of course. It happened gradually. Some people had been completely blind for years by that point; others could still see relatively well. But everyone agreed on the need for an official date. So we picked a day in late summer, the day of a solar eclipse. Would have been a good metaphor, I suppose, for those few who were able to see it. There were celebrations around the globe. Governments, media, and the entertainment industry all agreed it should be a joyous occasion, a party atmosphere. Audio fireworks exploded noisily over Times Square.

Everyone thought there would be catastrophes, that nuclear power plants would explode, that airplanes would fall out of the sky, that society would crumble. To be honest, we were expecting a wave of suicides once people began to notice the change.

It reminded us old folks of Y2K: so anticlimactic. Everyone just got drunk, had a party, and then got on with their lives.

You were born just a few weeks later. You've already adapted in ways we never would have thought of. I guess it's not even adaptation anymore; it's just progress, plain and simple.

Did you know I used to have to put on makeup every day so that my face would only reflect certain frequencies of light? Now romance is all about touch and smell and words. Don't tell your grandfather I said this, but it's better this way.

A lot of things are better now.

Headshot

@JMitcherCNN: Corporal, first of all, let me thank you for agreeing to this interview. By now, all of America has seen the footage of your amazing headshot last week. Could you tell us the story, in your own words?

@CplPetersUSMC: Well, sure, Jim. As you know, things went kinda crazy after I made that kill. I'm pushing 12k followers now. At the time, the most I'd ever had online at once was . . . maybe a couple dozen? Fact is, there were only two people with me when it happened— @PatriotRiot2000 and @FrendliGhost. This was the night of the assault on Peshawar, remember? So half the nation was following the boys from First Airborne. No one wanted to miss a jump like that. I appreciate all the fans who've been with me since the beginning, but I want to give credit where it's due. It was just me, Riot, and Ghost that night.

@JMitcherCNN: Interesting. So you didn't even have quorum for engagement?

@CplPetersUSMC: No, sir. Not at first. But that night, I wasn't even worrying about quorum. It was just a routine patrol, and we weren't expecting any trouble. I was just chatting with Ghost and Riot. Both of those dudes have always had my back with nav and sitreps and shit like that. But they were also just there when I needed someone to talk to, you know? That's even more important sometimes. When you're in the middle of a war zone, it's nice the hear the voice of some suburban kid from Detroit in your headset.

@JMitcherCNN: So how many other soldiers were taking part in this patrol?

@CplPetersUSMC: It was a six-man squad, but the tactical-scale guys had split us up to cover more ground. Ghost and Riot both thought that was dumb, but they'd been outvoted in the war room. When the numbers are small, bad ideas can get through more easily. That's the whole point of quorum. I admit, we were doing a bit of trash-talking. They told me there were a lot of tac-scale folks online who had never even really followed a soldier. They just spend all their time zoomed out, looking at satellite feeds, moving us around like chess pieces. I'm not saying that's wrong, but it can be dangerous. No one who's spent time with a soldier on patrol would have made that kind of call.

@JMitcherCNN: So it was just you alone in an alley. No backup.

@CplPetersUSMC: That's right. So then Riot notices this big black car parked in the alley. It was dark as hell in there. All the streetlights were out, so I didn't notice it. But Riot, he's a real tech-head. He has my feed running in infrared, thermal, and laser gated, each in a separate window. He don't miss much. And he's from Detroit, so he knows his cars. Anyway, it was a Lincoln. Most of the cars here are these shitty Soviet models from the '70s. Ain't that the ultimate irony? You can tell the guys on the most-wanted list 'cause they all drive American cars.

@JMitcherCNN: So you knew someone important was nearby.

@CplPetersUSMC: Well, we suspected. Ghost is looking at the satellite heat maps, pulling up floor plans, checking the locations of windows. I knew I couldn't just storm in there by myself, but Ghost and Riot didn't trust the guys in the war room, so they wanted to wait before calling in the cavalry. Those tac-scale yahoos would probably just send the squad in, guns blazing, just for the thrill of it. So Ghost guides me into this bombed-out office building across the street. I hoof it up five stories till I'm level with the building opposite. Sure enough, a light is on, and I can see into the room. There are six or seven bearded dudes there with AKs slung over their shoulders. It looks like they're arguing, and for a while, I think they're going to shoot each other and save me the bother, but then another guy comes in. You can tell just by looking at him that he's some sort of head honcho—the owner of the car. I didn't recognize him myself. I ain't no racist, but with those beards, they all look kinda the same. Riot, on the other hand, boots up some face-recognition software and IDs him, lickety-split, as Jaques al-Adil.

@JMitcherCNN: The Jack of Clubs.

@CplPetersUSMC: Exactly. This guy's a face card. One of the top ten most-wanted terrorists in the world, and I'm sitting in a window across the street from him, lined up for a perfect headshot.

@JMitcherCNN: But . . .

@CplPetersUSMC: But, as I mentioned, I didn't have quorum, so I couldn't take the shot. Legally. So Ghost and Riot jump on their social networks and try to get the word out. Any patriotic American would upvote a shot like that, but we just didn't have enough bodies in the room. Of course all their friends are watching the assault in Peshawar and not checking their messages. So you know what they do? Riot goes and wakes up his parents, and Ghost fetches his little sister and her boyfriend. Now, Riot's parents are real traditionalists who have never followed a soldier in their lives. Riot's always complaining about them, going on about how they're not upholding their responsibilities as citizens. They're old-timers, see? Got no interest in direct democracy.

@JMitcherCNN: Were they registered to vote?

@CplPetersUSMC: No! That's the thing. I think they were pre-screened through their driver's licenses or whatnot, but they certainly weren't registered for this theater. So I can hear Riot walking them through registration, trying to convince them how important this is, and they're trying to calm him down and typing their email addresses wrong and having to start again, just like any other old folks. Have to laugh at it all now.

@JMitcherCNN: I'm guessing it wasn't so funny at the time.

@CplPetersUSMC: It wasn't. But get this: the situation at Ghost's place is even worse. His sister is a hippie. A real peacenik, you know? She doesn't want anything to do with war. So I can hear him talking philosophy to her, trying to convince her to do the right thing for freedom and democracy just this once. And meanwhile I'm waiting with my rifle cocked and Jaques al-Adil's head in the middle of my sights. I've got to admit, Jim, I was sorely tempted to pull the trigger and just live with the consequences. But I thought to myself, If I shoot now, I'm no better than he is. I'm here as a representative of my country. If I shoot without a quorum of consenting citizens, as the rules of engagement demand, then I'm no longer defending freedom and democracy; I'm just another terrorist.

@JMitcherCNN: Strong words, Corporal.

@CplPetersUSMC: Well, if I didn't believe them, I never would have enlisted.

@JMitcherCNN: So what happened next?

@CplPetersUSMC: Well, then I hear gunfire coming from the next street over. I found out later that it was just Samuels and Gonzales showing off for some kids, but Ghost and Riot were too busy to keep me updated at this point, so it scared the hell out of me at the time. And it scared al-Adil and the rest of the folks around that table. They kill the lights and hit the floor. A minute later, I see the front door of the building open and four figures sprint to the Lincoln. One of them is al-Adil, and he gets in the back seat. My HUD was still only showing Ghost and Riot online, but just as the car was pulling away, three more followers blipped into existence. I had quorum. Now they just needed to upvote engagement. The car was already turning the corner of the street when the votes came through. Five out of five upvotes. Ghost had persuaded his sister's boyfriend to log in and vote. I couldn't even see al-Adil by this point. All I could see was the car, but I had seen him climb into the back right-hand seat, so I aimed for where I thought his head would be.

@JMitcherCNN: And the rest is history.

@CplPetersUSMC: And the rest is history. Although it would never have gone so viral if Samuels hadn't been just around the corner. He was the one who saw all the gore. It's his POV feed that's trending. Over 10M now, I think.

@JMitcherCNN: But seeing yours makes the shot all the more astonishing. I encourage all our followers to watch Cpl Peters's POV of the shot. If it had been a second later . . .

@CplPetersUSMC: Ghost and Riot have both made their screenfeeds public too. Be sure to check them out. Couldn't have done it without them.

@JMitcherCNN: So how do you think your job will change now that you have thousands of fans?

@CplPetersUSMC: Well, I certainly won't have trouble making quorum anymore . . . ROFL. On the one hand, it feels great to have the support of so many patriotic citizens behind me. But it'll be harder to have one-on-one chats with my followers. I'll do what I can to keep that personal connection. I've already set up a private channel for Ghost and Riot, so they'll always be able to talk to me directly, no matter how

The World of Dew and Other Stories

much chatter is going down. How will it change the job? I guess we'll just have to wait and see.

@JMitcherCNN: Just one more question, Corporal, and then I'll let you go. Sergeant Pearson's recent court-martial has sparked a grass-roots campaign to eliminate quorum altogether. Do you wish you had had more leeway? More freedom to act on your own initiative?

@CplPetersUSMC: Well, that's a great question, Jim. A lot of the older guys in the unit complain a lot about the whole direct-democracy thing, but I think I like things the way they are. Maybe if I had missed the shot, I would feel differently, but it seems to me that getting your folks out of bed to vote and debating philosophy with your sister before letting a soldier take a shot—that's how it should work. That's democracy.

@JMitcherCNN: Well said, Corporal. And thank you for your service.

Anxiety Boy and the Confidence Men

EVERY SUPERHERO HAS AN ORIGIN STORY. MINE BEGINS IN Mr. Callahan's ninth-grade English class. I knew that Steve Crouch was going to beat me up after school, so my guts were boiling with dread. It was that hair-trigger sloshing that usually only comes very early in the morning when I have easy access to the toilet. At school, it was a living nightmare, a purgatory of clench and sweat. I could have raised my hand and asked for permission to go to the bathroom, but that would only have attracted attention. And attention was the last thing I wanted.

"Mr. Yonge?" Mr. Callahan's voice came out of nowhere. He was suddenly standing over my desk, glaring down at me through his bifocals.

"Y-yes?"

The class erupted in laughter. I had only uttered one word, but it was something stupid and wrong.

"I would *advise* you to start paying attention, Oliver. I ask again, Why does Hamlet pretend to be mad?"

"I don't know," I mumbled.

Mr. Callahan sighed. "Well, why do you think? There's no wrong answer here, Oliver."

"I don't know," I said again, looking down at my desk, willing Mr. Callahan to drop the question. Every moment of the interaction drew more of the intolerable heat of attention. My stomach lurched. I was sure I was about to shit my pants.

But that's not what happened. Not quite. Something did come out of me, but it came directly out of my belly, like the Chestburster scene in *Alien* or that thing the Care Bears do. It burst out of me and rearranged the world, pushing things around and shifting the currents of attention.

Impossibly, no one else seemed to notice.

Just a moment before, Mr. Callahan was going to press the question, force me to make something up. I was sure of it. But the thing that had emerged from my gut changed that.

Mr. Callahan just sighed again and moved on to the next desk. "What about you, Elizabeth? Why do you think Hamlet feigns madness?"

As the heat of attention faded, I realized that my belly felt a little less twisted up.

* * *

Invisibility would be my superpower of choice. Other kids might have chosen superstrength or superspeed, but I didn't want to beat up or outrun my tormenters. I just wanted to be able to disappear, to fade into the cool gray background of the school and go about my day entirely unnoticed.

The closest I ever came to achieving this dream was after the intermediate band Christmas concert. We were halfway home when I realized I had left my keys in my bassoon case. Mom turned the car around, and we went back. The custodians were still there, buffing the floors of the main hallway. They ignored me as I made my way to the music room.

Everything was quiet that night. Most of the lights in the school were off, and the long locker-lined corridors lay inert, free of menace for once. It was as if the school had relaxed its muscles or let out a breath it had been holding all day. That was how I imagined invisibility would feel.

I tried to keep that feeling inside me all night in the hopes that it would persist into the next school day. But by morning, it had faded.

There was no way it could flourish under the inimical fluorescent lights of Central Consolidated High School.

* * *

I came home after school with bruises on my ribs from Steve Crouch's boots. The beating hadn't been too bad, because Mr. Gary had come around the corner in the middle of it, and Steve had to pretend to be helping me up. But as he leaned in, he whispered that he wasn't finished with me and that I would get it twice as bad the next day.

"Are you all right, honey?" Mom said at suppertime. "You seem out of sorts this evening."

"Just tired, Mom. Think I'll have an early night."

"You're not ill, are you, sweetie?"

"No. Not ill." I smiled and took a big mouthful of meatloaf so I wouldn't have to talk anymore.

* * *

I was in bed by nine o'clock, but I knew I wouldn't be able to get to sleep until at least midnight. That gave me three hours to focus on my worry. I began by imagining the beating I would receive the next day after school. There was no escaping Steve Crouch. He was a faster runner than me, and he had spies at every exit. I pressed a finger against my tender ribs and imagined his boot connecting with the same spot again and again.

The worry bloomed in my belly, a dreadful quivering that made me wince and grit my teeth. It was like an engine starting up, shuddering as it began to turn over and pick up speed. Once it was running, it fed itself. Worry about Steve Crouch led to worry about general humiliation, about shitting myself in public, about being mocked and hated by other kids at school, about never being loved, about global warming and nuclear war and pandemics.

I didn't know exactly what had happened in Mr. Callahan's class, but I knew my worry had changed the world.

* * *

By morning, I was ready.

It lay in my belly all day, writhing and squirming like a pit of snakes. I fed it intermittently, giving it a snack of remembered humiliation or imagined terror.

Steve himself gave it a boost when he passed me in the hall and lunged at me, laughing as I jumped and banged my hip on the water fountain.

By the time the bell rang, it was ready to burst its banks. It was all I could do to get from the locker to the front entrance. My legs quivered, and my bladder ached, even though I had just peed. I let myself be carried along by the current of students flowing toward the doors and freedom.

There was Steve Crouch, sitting on the low wall in the front parking lot, chatting with Sue Palgrove. He saw me as soon as I emerged from the school. I'm sure of it. He looked directly at me and nodded as if to say, "The time has come."

I let out a quiet moan as it flooded out of me, that highly pressurized anxiety. It was physical and violent, like a judo throw. It shoved and prodded at reality, pulling at the fabric of things, rearranging the world in its rush to escape. But nobody noticed.

Here's how it happened: Steve Crouch saw me, made eye contact, stood up, began to approach. But then my anxiety changed things. And Steve Crouch changed his mind.

He looked suddenly confused, as if he had forgotten what he was about to do. Then he went back to the wall and continued flirting with Sue Palgrove.

As soon as I was out of sight, I broke into a run. My belly felt weightless. I was giddy and breathing hard.

This changed everything.

I had the power to change the world.

* * *

Over the next three weeks, I stopped a dozen humiliations. I worried that Mr. Grohl would yell at me for not doing my homework, but that day, in an unbelievable break with tradition, he forgot to collect it. I worried that Gary Peterson would pull my trunks down or push me into the girls' changeroom during swim class, but Gary was sick on swim day. I worried that Jenny Pilgrim would yell at me because she got caught copying my test, but she actually apologized for almost getting *me* in trouble.

In each case, it was my worry that changed things. A fluttering, burning, twisting blob emerged from my guts and made things different.

It only failed once, and that was my own fault. It failed because I became complacent. It was school-spirit day. Instead of going to afternoon classes, we all gathered in the gym in our yellow-and-blue T-shirts and played games.

I always dreaded spirit days. Without the structure and routine of the classroom, I had to be on high alert. I would be a target for bullies who weren't even in my grade. But this time I knew my worry would save me. So, of course, it didn't.

When I saw Don Fakebern barreling toward me holding a medicine ball, I tried to rouse the creature in my guts. I was sure it would shift his trajectory ever so slightly, forcing him to collide with Johnny Mavis or Jo Huan. But I found nothing there. The place where the creature lurked was empty. I just felt fine.

The medicine ball broke my nose, and I had to be taken to the hospital. As I waited in Emergency, I worried that I would be hideously deformed for the rest of my life, that fragments of bone had been driven into my brain, that the doctor would demand a urine sample and I would be too worried to go.

But when Dr. Glenn saw me at last, my worry surged into the world, straightening cartilage, staunching blood flow, changing the prognosis. Dr. Glenn prodded at my nose, gave me some Tylenol, and told me I would be back to normal in a few days.

I never made that mistake again. From then on, whenever I started to think my worry would save me, a feeling of despair formed in my gut. My own confidence in my powers became a new source of anxiety. And, just like that, a new wave of reinforcements would arrive, like Gandalf leading the Rohirrim at the Battle of Helm's Deep. And whenever I began to grow too confident that those reinforcements would save me, a fresh wave of anxiety would crash over me at the thought. Confidence itself became a source of worry, a double agent waiting for a chance to betray me. And that worry reassured me, which made me anxious. And so on.

* * *

I wasn't surprised when the men in dark blazers came to collect me. Somehow, they knew. Somehow, I knew they would know.

They knew I had been messing with reality. They knew about Mr. Callahan and Steve Crouch and Jenny Pilgrim. They even knew about the time I was worried that someone would knock on the door of the stall in the basement washroom. They knew that for a few blessed moments, I was alone in the room and could pee in peace. They knew that it was thanks to my worry changing the world.

My mother cried as they led me away to the black SUV, but she told me she was proud of me. She told me she knew I would make her even prouder.

The men's names were Mr. Gin and Dr. Cee. They took me to an empty, bland room in a nameless office building outside Washington, DC. They showed me photos of a North Korean ICBM. They told me it was being prepared for launch. They told me it could hit any city in the United States. They even showed me a classified video of the launch site, taken by a spy satellite.

"You must understand why we have brought you here, Mr. Yonge," said Mr. Gin. "You have a gift. The United States has need of that gift."

"*Humanity* has need of that gift," said Dr. Cee.

So I worried. I worried in a hotel room with secret service agents standing guard outside the door. I worried about a nuke hurtling through the thermosphere toward Washington or New York or the Pentagon.

Or rather, I tried.

The prospect of millions of people being burned to a crisp and the Eastern Seaboard being reduced to a radioactive wasteland just didn't seem particularly worrying. Not compared to someone walking in on me while peeing.

I switched on the TV to try to find something that would trigger my anxiety. A horror movie or a family drama or Gordon Ramsay yelling at someone. But all I found was a comfortable slurry of news and cartoons and home-renovation shows. I wasn't worried at all. I was just bored.

A good person would have been worried for all those lives about to be lost. My own pathetic selfishness is what saved us all. I was worried not that people would die but that I would be blamed. It formed in my belly like food poisoning and then rushed out into the world.

The next morning, the headlines read, "Launch Postponed. Doomsday Averted."

Men in fancy suits arrived at my hotel room to congratulate me.

"Are you hungry?" asked Dr. Cee. "I'll get us some breakfast."

"Can I go home now?" I asked.

"Not yet," Mr. Gin said. "We have more work for you."

Dr. Cee came back with a value meal from McDonald's, and Mr. Gin told me about a famine in South Sudan. He opened his laptop and showed me images of malnourished children with distended bellies.

As I ate my Big Mac, I stared at the images and imagined how disgusted everyone would be with me if I didn't prevent this. I imagined my mom, my teachers, and my classmates all shaking their heads in disappointment.

"More worried about himself than he is about starving children." I didn't imagine anyone specific saying these words. It was just a general sentiment shared by all good people. It turned my insides to liquid.

By the next week, aid shipments were being distributed throughout the affected region, and crops were making a miraculous recovery.

That was how I spent the summer and fall of that year. Each morning, Mr. Gin and Dr. Cee would present me with a problem, and I would stoke my boilers with anxiety, forcing great shovelfuls of worry into my guts. I was never worried about the thing they wanted me to worry about, only about how everyone would see me if I failed. But it worked.

Occasionally, some doctors and scientists would visit to take blood samples and put me through MRI scanners while I worried. I worried that I would become claustrophobic in the machines, so of course I didn't. But then I worried that my lack of worry would screw up their experiments and they'd be mad.

"Are you anxious?" asked the scientists.

"Yes," I told them.

"Good," they said. Which made me relax and threw off their tests, which upset them, which made me worry some more, which produced the results they wanted.

I stopped a nasty virus from going global. I diverted the course of a hurricane. I caused a brutal dictator to abdicate and transfer power peacefully. I suppose I felt a certain amount of pride. But I couldn't afford to let it go to my head. I knew I had to stay one step ahead of the agents of complacency. Every success made my job harder and the worry more difficult to sustain.

That worried me.

The hotel room began to feel like a prison, and I began to worry that I would never go home. So, of course, the worry beast writhed, and my mom came to collect me the next day. Mr. Gin and Dr. Cee said that I had proven my loyalty and that I was free to continue my work from home. They still visited every day or two with a new mission, a new catastrophe waiting to happen.

But then a new worry crept into my belly. It started out small and insignificant, but it grew bigger by the day, until it became the main thing I spent my time worrying about.

I worried that I would never be normal, that I would never go back to school. I worried that I would spend the rest of my life as a refinery for weapons-grade anxiety.

* * *

The gang came in the night. They scaled the side of the house, forced open my bedroom window, and bundled me up in a large blanket.

Being kidnapped is terrifying. But terror is a different beast from worry. It doesn't project into the future. It happens *now*. So I couldn't stop it from happening.

The last thing I felt was a syringe pricking my arm. And then nothing.

When I woke up, I found myself in some sort of clubhouse. There were comfy couches against the walls, a pool table in the middle of the room, and a wet bar in one corner. The gang members lounged around, chatting and laughing. They were a little older than me. Young men and women with cool haircuts and cans of beer.

"He's coming to," someone said. "How are you feeling, buddy?"

I tried to speak, but my mouth was dry and sticky.

"Get him some water! Help him up."

I was lying on one of the couches, but now two of the other gang members helped me sit up. "Who . . . ?" I croaked. "Where . . . ?"

"Don't worry," said a guy with a beard and dark glasses. "We'll explain everything."

"We know about the work you were doing for Special Operations," said a woman chewing a toothpick. "We know what they forced you to do. We're here to help you get your life back."

"What do you mean?" I rubbed my eyes and took a sip of the water they brought me. "You kidnapped me."

"Had to," said the woman. "Otherwise you would have worried us out of existence. Had to make it a surprise that you didn't have time to worry about."

"I'm worried now," I said.

"No doubt," said the woman. "But you're worried that we're a gang of criminals or we're holding you for ransom or we're going to torture you or something. None of that's true."

The guy with the beard smiled at me. "We're the Confidence Men," he said. "We're here to cure you."

I spent the next week hanging out with the Confidence Men. We played pool, drank Coke, and watched movies. It was kind of great. They thought I was funny. And I could tell they were laughing *with* me and not at me. They understood my jokes, even when I screwed up telling them. When I told them I loved video games, they all high-fived and brought out a Nintendo Switch. They weren't just humoring me either. You could tell they genuinely loved gaming and loved me for loving gaming. They called me *buddy* and *boss* and *champ*. They let me try sips of beer. One of them even gave me my first kiss during a game of truth or dare.

They had explained everything to my mom. We Skyped a few times, and she told me that it sounded like the Confidence Men were doing what was best for me, that she loved me and she would see me soon.

"We've got to starve it," explained Cory, the leader of the Confidence Men. "The thing inside you. If it doesn't have any worry to feed on, it'll wither away and die."

"OK," I said. Maybe I should have been worried about the thing dying, about my work for Dr. Cee and Mr. Gin. But I just wanted to play another game of *Mario Kart* with the Confidence Men.

In many ways, the time I spent in that clubhouse was the happiest of my life. For the first time, I felt normal. For the first time, I felt understood. For the first time, I had friends. And I got pretty good at pool too.

So of course I began to worry about my time there coming to an end. I worried that all of this would be over and I would never see the Confidence Men again.

And then it was all over, and I never saw the Confidence Men again. They said there were others who needed them, that I had succeeded beyond their wildest expectations and that I could go back to being a normal kid.

"It wasn't us," said Cory. These were his parting words to me. "*You* did this. We just helped you see what was truly inside you all along." He looked me in the eyes when he said this and held my gaze a little too long after he had finished speaking.

* * *

After the Confidence Men let me out of the clubhouse, I worried that Mr. Gin and Dr. Cee would take me back to that hotel room in Washington, DC. And they did.

They showed up at my home with an armored car and a dozen security officers. They said it was for my own protection. My mom seemed annoyed. She was getting tired of having me whisked away by shadowy strangers. But Mr. Gin and Dr. Cee seemed relieved to have me back. They showed me a video of a meteor heading toward the earth.

I worried. I swear I did. If anything, I worried *more* than normal, because I was worried it wouldn't work anymore. I worried that the Confidence Men really had cured me.

The meteor hit a city in the Midwest and killed thirty-five thousand people.

* * *

I'm back home now. Back with my mom. Back in school. Mr. Gin and Dr. Cee tried a few more times before they gave up on me. They yelled at me, just like I worried they would. They called me a selfish child and said I was letting everyone down. But it did no good.

I still feel awful when a nuclear power plant explodes or a regional border dispute turns into an ugly war or Steve Crouch threatens to beat me up. But there's nothing I can do about it. I worry just as much as ever, but my worry stays nested in my guts, where it belongs.

And that's my origin story. I guess also whatever is the opposite of an origin story too. My postcredits sequence? Sometimes, I worry that Mr. Gin and Dr. Cee were the good guys all along and the Confidence Men were a band of supervillains. But it doesn't matter what I worry about anymore. And that's a relief.

Hospice

THE BANSHEE IS WAILING. THERE'S GOING TO BE A DEATH tonight.

We never know for sure who it's going to be, but my money's on Mrs. Johnson. Over the last few days, something's felt different about her. She's already elsewhere, no longer present in her crumbling body.

Some of the other staff complain about the banshee, blaming her for headaches and nightmares, but she's only doing her job. A death takes a lot out of you, no matter how many you've seen before, and her warning gives me time to get ready, to prepare the paperwork and armor my heart.

I spend the night turning Mrs. Johnson every few hours, swabbing her dry mouth, rubbing Vaseline onto her desiccated skin. I can hear the fluid in her lungs when she breathes. It can't be long now.

And yet by the end of my shift, Mrs. Johnson is still breathing. She even gives me a weak smile. I perform my final rounds in a panic, frantic that someone else has passed while I've been focused on Mrs. Johnson. But no. There are pulses all around.

It's raining as I sign out and climb onto my bicycle. The banshee is still wailing, but her shift is nearly over too, and she's a stickler for rules. I guess she just got it wrong this time.

With drooping eyelids, I pull out of the parking lot, and her wail is drowned out by the whoosh and roar of rush-hour traffic on slick streets.

The Monster

WAS THE MONSTER CREATED OR DISCOVERED? THERE'S NO easy answer to that. We dragged it screaming from the Stew, that unknowable portal that the eggheads at Oak Ridge cobbled together from quantum physics and sheer hubris.

For the first few years, it spent every waking hour wailing from its thousand throats, but nowadays it just weeps quietly in the containment field, tears oozing from those hypnotic, light-sensitive fins. Some say it's lonely; others say it's homesick. The scientists say we shouldn't project human emotions onto it, that it's probably just purging its body of unfamiliar earthly toxins.

The media is obsessed with the monster. It's been on the front page of every newspaper, an unwilling guest on every talk show, a fashion icon, an ambiguous political talking point.

The right doesn't know what to think. On the one hand, the monster is clearly an abomination, a horrifying corruption of intelligent design, a punishment for playing God. On the other hand, what are we supposed to do? Kill it?

The left is just as confused. They campaign to have its sentience recognized, to give it human rights. But what are we supposed to do? Release it? Even if we had a way to render it harmless, the days of the rampage are still too fresh in our memories.

So we argue about it, and feed it, and watch it grow, and wait for the inevitable day when we can no longer keep it contained.

Practice

I FIND THE VIOLIN AT ELSEVIER'S MUSICAL CURIOSITIES ON Mott Street. I wander in on a whim seeking refuge from a sudden cold rain and stay for hours, bewitched by the sprawling shop.

The violin lies in a case marked *Special Acquisitions,* and a gnome-like salesman encourages me to try it out. I haven't played since high school, but as soon as I raise the instrument to my chin, it all comes flooding back—the muscle memory, the skid and jump of the bow across the strings. It's like hugging a beloved friend whom I haven't seen in years.

The world holds its breath as I play. I saw out the gigues and sarabands that Mr. Brochure taught me in senior music and the horas that I learned from my great-aunt Borislava. My playing is rusty and rough, but I'm in heaven. Those jagged, sloppy melodies feel vital and alive. I hadn't realized how much I miss that feeling.

When I pull the violin out from under my chin, I'm not sure how much time has passed. It felt like hours, but the salesman is still standing there, nodding politely.

"Go ahead," he says, motioning for me to keep playing.

"Oh, my mind's made up," I tell him. "I'll take it."

I leave the shop with a smile on my face.

* * *

The next weekend, my roommate, Sally, emerges from the darkness of her room with big headphones dangling from her neck. "Well, go on, then. Aren't you going to play it for me?"

"What do you mean?" I'm wiping rosin from the fingerboard with a soft rag.

"You've been raving about that thing all week, but I haven't heard you play it once."

I stare at Sally for a second, trying to work out if she's being sarcastic. I love her to bits, but Sally doesn't always think in the same way as other people. "What are you talking about, Sal? I spent all afternoon playing."

"All afternoon? We only just had lunch."

I roll my eyes. "You've been gaming, right?" I point at her headphones. "You always lose track of time when you're jacked into *Ever-Crack*. No wonder you didn't hear me."

"I haven't been gaming," Sally replies a little defensively. "We finished lunch, like, five minutes ago." She gives me a funny look. "Are you OK, Barb?"

"Seriously!" I laugh. "I've been playing for hours. It's already . . ." The living room clock shows 1:07. "Huh. Must've stopped."

But the clock is still ticking, and in the kitchen, the leftover pasta is still steaming.

*   *   *

Here's the thing: *Book One of the Fitzwilliam Violin Method* contains thirty-two melodic études of increasing difficulty. Each one takes *at least* two minutes to play, so if you play the book straight through, without ever going back over anything, you're talking an hour of playing, minimum. These are facts. I did the math longhand, multiplying the number of bars by the number of beats in each bar, then dividing by the tempo. I would have just timed them, but my watch is acting up. So are all the clocks in the house. My metronome isn't working either, but I'm careful not to rush. If anything, I play the pieces *slower* than intended.

And yet I can start playing at 5:59 p.m., run all thirty-two études from top to bottom, and be finished in time to catch the six o'clock news.

I just don't get it. So I ask Sally to time me on her digital watch. She has one of those big clunky ones from the '80s, and she seems pleased that I'm willing to acknowledge its superiority over my modern Timex.

The watch beeps. "Go!"

Sally keeps her eyes on the digits the whole time I'm playing, her finger poised over the button, as if this experiment is going to need split-second precision.

I blast through a couple of gigues from memory, then lower my violin.

"Are you ready?" says Sally. "Clock is running."

"That's good enough. How long did that take?"

Sally just blinks at me. Her eyebrows knit in confusion, so I go over to her and grab her wrist.

The seconds steadily tick by on the face of the watch: 06 . . . 07 . . . 08 . . . 09 . . . The minutes remain at 00.

"Let's try again," I say, my voice quivery and soft.

"We haven't tried once yet."

"Just . . . humor me, OK?"

I stand by her side and watch her reset the timer. I hear the beep and watch the seconds begin to count up: . . . 01 . . . 02 . . . 03 . . .

And when I begin to play, the seconds stop. The number 03 just hangs out there on the display, as if it's got nowhere better to be. Even the tiny hundredths-of-a-second digits have come to a dead halt at 79.

I keep playing, my eyes glued to the watch face. I'm just playing random slow notes at this point, not really thinking about it.

My eyes wander from the watch to Sally. She's unnaturally still. I can see it now that I'm standing close to her. Her right hand hangs in the air at an awkward angle, frozen halfway between her wrist and her hip. Her lips are slightly parted, as if she's about to say something. She's paralyzed and—oh my god—not breathing.

As soon as I stop playing, movement returns to the world—04 . . . 05 . . . 06—and Sally starts to breathe again. Her hand drops to her side, and she hooks a thumb through the belt loop of her jeans.

She looks up at me quizzically. "Whenever you're ready?"

I put the violin down carefully, as if it's a loaded weapon. "Sal," I whisper. "Something weird is going on."

* * *

I bring my fiddle to Central Park on a blustery day. The trees are noisy and writhing. Traffic on Fifth Avenue honks and blares.

But as I start to play, the world falls still, and all is silent save for my violin.

Over by the benches, a pigeon hangs in the air, midtakeoff. It looks startled and ridiculous, a foot from the ground, its legs dangling uselessly beneath it.

A Coke can hovers just above the rim of a garbage can. Three feet away, a man stands with his hand outstretched, his fingers slightly curled from imparting spin to the can. His brows are knitted with concentration. His aim isn't perfect, but the can's going to go in—just.

A jogger is caught midstride. She balances on the ball of her left foot, leaning forward at an impossible angle. Physics dictates that she must either thrust her left foot forward to catch her weight or topple to the ground. But she does neither. She waits there, defying gravity.

It's so peaceful, here in this motionless Manhattan.

I play a meandering adagio, half-remembered and half-improvised. It doesn't seem to matter what I play. A single note is enough to stop time, but I like to fill the silence with something more than that. It feels pure, this private music.

I yearn to stroll the streets while I play. I would like to explore this instant in the life of New York City, but as soon as I put bow to string, I find myself rooted to the spot, my legs frozen in time, like the pigeon, and the jogger, and the Coke can. In vague terror, I wonder if I'll age faster above the waist than below. Will my boobs age and sag while my butt remains young and firm?

I bring my piece to its end. The bird flaps clumsily in the air. The Coke can bounces off the rim and rattles into the garbage. The jogger huffs and puffs on her way by. The world is full of noise and motion again.

* * *

I convince Sally of what I can do by memorizing a page of a book. She opens one of her fantasy novels to a random chapter, and I begin to play slow scales while I read. Reading and playing at the same time feels like rubbing your belly while patting your head; it's a little counterintuitive but not impossible. So I memorize a page and then recite it back to her verbatim.

We videotape the whole thing using my brother's old camcorder and watch the tape on Sally's portable TV.

Here's what happens: Sally stands in front of me with a copy of *The Dwarf Holds of Glom-Helding*, her finger in a page. I raise the violin to my chin, and she opens the book in front of my face. Then I touch my bow to the strings.

That's it. I don't even appear to glance at the book. I just lower my bow again and start reciting. "A single swing of Groondool's ax was all it took to fell the great oak tree. He felt sorrow at its loss, but the timber would be invaluable to the armory. The trolls were advancing again, coming up from the foothills to raid the mountain passes and harry the caravans that brought gold down from Glom-Helding. All-out war was inevitable."

"Holy shit!" says Sally before I've done even a paragraph. "Can I have a go?"

Sally saws away at the violin, but nothing happens. Or rather, something *does* happen. What happens is exactly what's supposed to happen when a person plays a violin for the first time. She makes hideous screeches and yowls.

"Damn. It didn't work, did it?"

"'Fraid not."

Sally looks at me as if I've cheated her out of something. I just shrug, but secretly I'm relieved. My secret, still moments remain mine alone.

* * *

"What a shitty superpower," Sally says later that night over beer. "If you could move around, it'd be like teleportation. That'd be wicked."

"I know, I know. What am I supposed to do with it? I can memorize stuff. I can think things through . . . but I can't really *do* anything, can I?"

"If you're ever on *Jeopardy!* you could ace the Daily Double."

I laugh. "I'd still need to know the answer. It just buys me a little more time. And they'd have to let me have my violin on set!"

"Well, cramming for tests would be easier," Sally suggests. "In school, you always left assignments till the last minute. Now you'll have all the time you need."

"That's true. But it's kind of a hassle to play the whole time I'm studying. I can't even turn pages while time is stopped. And my arm gets tired pretty quick."

"Hey, at least you can practice without the neighbors complaining."

"That's true." I raise my glass. "To practicing!"

After that, we don't really discuss the violin much. You've got to be open-minded to live with a roommate, and Sally is more open-minded than most. She accepts people as they are, and expects to be accepted in return. She has a collection of colorful vibrators that she keeps on our bookshelf; I have a violin that can stop time. Both took some getting used to, but neither is a big deal in the grand scheme of things.

*   *   *

Christmas is coming, and Mott Street is irritatingly cheery. The little cafés advertise eggnog lattes, and lights wrap every lamppost. Holiday jingles blast from every store, and there are crowds of jostling tourists and herds of students from NYU. But I can window-shop in peace by playing my violin, setting up outside each store in turn like the world's least-successful busker.

As a kid, I used to raise money for my local soup kitchen by playing carols outside the liquor store at this time of year. Merry shoppers would empty their pockets into my case. There's something about a child on a violin that breaks through people's defenses. But nobody will ever give me money for what I play on this violin, no matter how good I get.

Elsevier's is located just north of Prince Street, beside a grungy café called the Brass Spittoon. It's a tall narrow building, set back from the street on an irregular lot. It's a surprising site in lower Manhattan, where the buildings muscle right up to the sidewalks, shoving their merchandise in the faces of passersby.

It *was* a surprising site, anyway. When I arrive at the address, Elsevier's is gone. The Brass Spittoon is still there, smelling of old coffee, but beside it is a large church advertising the "only Catholic catacombs in Manhattan."

I must have made a wrong turn. The Brass Spittoon must be a chain. My memory must be faulty. So I check the business card inside my violin case:

Elsevier's Musical Curiosities
726 Mott Street, Manhattan
Open by Chance

I'm in the right place, but the shop is gone.

It's easy to believe that Elsevier's went out of business within the last two weeks, but I don't understand how it could have been replaced by a two-hundred-year-old church.

"Excuse me, ma'am?" I ask a nice-looking old lady. "How long has this church been here? I mean, has it always been at this location?"

"Yes, dear," she says. "The cathedral was built in the 1700s, I believe."

"So it wasn't . . . like . . . moved brick by brick from somewhere else?" I show her the business card and describe the instrument shop as best I can.

She just shrugs. "Must be a misprint, dear. Buildings don't just disappear."

* * *

It's nearly the year 2000, and I've come to Times Square with a million other people to watch the ball drop. I've got an invitation to a party over in Williamsburg, but I want to be here, among the glitz and tourists. What's the point of living in New York if you're just going to go to a house party on New Year's?

A doctor from Doctors Without Borders is on the big screen, and the crowd roars as she presses the button to start the ball's sixty-second descent.

We're packed in close, and I have to shove a little to get my case open and extract my violin.

"Ten, nine . . ." roars the crowd.

My scroll digs into someone's back, and she's turning to complain as I play my first note.

Seconds from a new millennium, a million people hold their breaths in Times Square. And I play "Auld Lang Syne" into the silence.

If the prophecies of doom are correct, then this could be my last moment of happiness. It's possible that nuclear reactors are going to explode and planes are about to fall from the sky because of old computer code that can't conceive of a time this far in the future. If that comes to pass, then this moment could be the last good moment for humanity. I feel a certain obligation to enjoy it, so I play a dozen verses, twisting as best I can to look into the eyes of the people around me as I play.

These people will remember this evening as a blur of color and noise. They'll remember the fireworks, the numb fingers, the huge puppets making their way down Broadway. But only I will remember the precise looks on their faces at three seconds to midnight.

When I'm done, I grin at the woman I poked and wish her happy new year. She grins back.

*   *   *

It's that moment that I remember. It's that moment in Times Square that comes back to me when I notice the airplane that shouldn't be there, flying too low and too fast over Manhattan.

I carry my violin with me everywhere these days. I rely on it the way I used to rely on cigarettes. I get it out when I'm overwhelmed, or stressed, or angry. I play on the subway and at work. I play whenever I'm running late. It doesn't make me any earlier, but it gives me time. It gives me space to breathe. And as a result, I'm getting good again. It's a shitty superpower, I know, but I'm grateful for it all the same.

So on that morning in September, I unsling my violin and yank it from its case, barely thinking. It's instinct by now. In moments of panic, I play, forcing the world to stand still while I get my shit together. And this is certainly a moment of panic.

The World of Dew and Other Stories

I fling my empty case to the ground as I raise the instrument to my chin. It bounces on its reinforced corner, and my violin sounds before it comes to rest. The case hangs in the air, about to strike the pavement again.

I gaze down Broadway, playing something simple. It's impossible to wrap my head around what I'm seeing. It's a long way away, but still much too close.

The stillness is almost unbearable. Instead of calming me, it heightens my anxiety. I feel the weight of this moment on my shoulders. All I have to do is stop, and everything will resolve itself, for better or for worse. As soon as I stop, my responsibility will have ended.

But I don't stop. The people on that airplane are about to die. That much is clear. Many others may die too. But as long as I keep playing, they will still be alive.

So I play and play, stretching the moment to the breaking point and beyond. I fight back waves of panic and force my arm to keep moving. It feels both important and useless.

It won't make a difference. I know that. How long can I keep this up before I drop from exhaustion? A few hours? A day? As soon as I stop, it will have all been pointless. The future is always there waiting, with infinite patience. It will wear me down. And when I break, all my stalling won't have made a lick of difference.

The only thing I get out of this is time to think, or pray. But I'm too rattled to think clearly, and I've never been a believer.

So I just play. I play the gigues and sarabands that Mr. Brochure taught me. I play the horas that I learned from my great-aunt Borislava. I play "Auld Lang Syne" and the violin part from Samuel Barber's "Adagio for Strings." I play scales and arpeggios and the thirty-two melodic études from *Book One of the Fitzwilliam Violin Method*. Before long, I realize that I'm not just playing; I'm *practicing*. And at this moment, practice feels important. It feels as though I'm laboring, erecting a bulwark against terror.

And that's when I think back to New Year's. We worried about airplanes being knocked out of the sky by a computer bug. We worried about civilization falling apart because of the ticking of time—not gradually but all at once. I think about how I stopped that ticking and memorized the faces of the people around me, just in case.

I think about buildings vanishing without a trace.

There was something triumphal about the celebrations that night. As lovers kissed and fireworks burst and bands played, we all felt that we had stared disaster in the face and won.

Will this moment turn out like that? It's impossible to say. But just in case, I'll keep practicing.

Foundation

THERE WERE THINGS MISSING FROM GABBLETON. THAT WAS how it seemed now, after all those years away. It was like playing Kim's Game with her brothers as a child. The old wooden tea tray, full of small objects—a thimble, a pencil, a model car, a box of matches, a sugar cube. And something missing. Something that had been there before. Something that Kate couldn't quite put her finger on.

Had there been a fruit-and-veg stall on this corner? A metal climbing frame in this playground? The health-food store was still there, and there was a new supermarket out by the highway, so Kate stocked up on food and household essentials. A mop and broom, vacuum-cleaner bags, enough food to last until they were finished, however long that would take. And some luxuries: chocolate, expensive coffee, beer and wine, fresh juices. This was a vacation, after all, and a reunion, and a goodbye party.

As children, they had always stopped in Gabbleton on their way home and bought groceries like this, mountains of them, enough to last months. If they were good, their father bought doughnuts to eat in the car. But Kate bought a bag of oranges instead.

It was that time of day that she liked best, just before dusk, the sun low on the horizon and everything golden. The rental car smoothed along, almost silent. There was no other traffic on the road. It would have been quicker to travel on Highway 101, but it hadn't existed when she was a child. Kate wanted to see the villages and the ocean. So she took the old Highway 1—recently renamed the Evangeline Trail by some tourism committee—with its blind hills, hidden driveways, and constantly changing speed limits. She drove with the vast power of the Bay of Fundy surging at her side.

Half an hour from town, the fields gave way to woodland, but the stone walls continued. Kate took an orange from the bag in the passenger seat and ripped the skin off in chunks with her teeth, spitting it back into the plastic bag. Deliciously bitter. Had her father been there, he would have started on one of his rambles: "That orange used to be just one object, but now you're dissecting it, multiplying it. Those pieces of peel aren't objects anymore at all—they're just garbage, metaphysical debris, to be done away with as quickly as possible. The flesh of the fruit is an object. Each segment is an object. Each pip is an object. But we're most comfortable with oranges when they're complete, skin and all. Such a nice, tidy, discrete unit. Entirely imaginary, of course."

There it was. The wide metal gate. And beyond it, the dirt road through the woods. The neighbors had always mistrusted them for their gate, considering them unfriendly and reclusive. She knew that there were rumors about her father in the nearby villages. Nobody knew what to make of this man who rarely left his house and lived alone with three children who did not go to school. But the locals had all been very kind to her that day. They remembered her, and everyone she spoke to seemed to have some story of a chance encounter with her father in which he had displayed generosity or kindness.

She used to love hanging on to the gate as her father opened it, riding it through its long slow arc. Now it was rusty and stiff, and it gave a shriek of protest as she forced it open. But then she was through. On her own land. Her own.

The sun had nearly set by the time the woods ended and she crested the little hill. There it was, in silhouette, the house she had grown up in. A grand cottage of lumber and thatch with green shuttered windows and two chimneys. The land about the house was wild. It had been left untended for years, but then it had always been like that. Her father had never attempted to create a lawn. He despised electric mowers, let alone ride-ons, so he had left the grounds to their own devices. Daisies and dandelions and clover thrived here, and Kate had an urge to run naked through it as she had when she was a baby, grass tickling her armpits.

On the far side of the house were the cliffs. They dropped thirty feet onto a stony beach and the Atlantic.

The spare key was still under the same rock where her father had left it. She had half expected it not to be there, as if his death should have erased all his actions. But there it was. It felt like communicating with the dead.

Kate let herself in the back door and went into every room, opening shutters and flicking switches, filling the house with light, chasing away all the shadows. To her surprise, the house didn't feel haunted. Just warmly, almost boringly, familiar.

It felt good to be back, but it brought on a forgotten teenage lethargy. In Montreal, she would have begun dusting and cleaning, putting the house in order for when her brother arrived. But now she decided to do as little as she could get away with. Michael could help her clean tomorrow. She just plugged in the fridge and put the perishables inside, then slumped on the couch with a bottle of beer and fell asleep there, full of memories.

* * *

Michael arrived the next morning in a van, which she heard before she saw. It was quiet here, just the ocean and the gulls. When Kate was a child, the sound of automobiles had always seemed rude and invasive, an unwelcome disturbance to their quiet world. Her father's friends arriving with their false laughter and peculiar smells. She and her brothers would gather at the upstairs window to keep an eye on the car as it approached. She went to that window now and perched on the sill.

The van was Kate's first hint that the plan had changed. Why would Michael need a van? She tried to imagine what was inside. Furniture? A canoe? His record collection? It didn't make sense. By the time it had pulled up to the house, there were more questions to be answered. There were other people in the van. She had explicitly told Michael not to bring Fiona, and he had agreed. This was a family matter. Kate stormed downstairs and threw open the front door.

Michael was the first to climb down from the cab of the van. He had grown a beard since the funeral, but he had the same boyhood smile that never left his lips. He ran to her, and they hugged tightly, rocking from foot to foot as if the force of the hug were overflowing and had to be released in this way.

With her chin pressed to his shoulder, Kate peered around Michael's neck and watched the others getting out of the van, stretching and lighting cigarettes. Nobody she recognized. She whispered loud, right in Michael's ear, "Who the *fuck* are those people, Michael? I thought we were going to do this together? Just the two of us?"

"Aw, c'mon, Kate. You know we can't," he whispered back. "It would take months with just the two of us. These guys are professionals. And better still, they all know Foundation. If we're going to do this, we may as well do it right."

Kate pulled away, her fingers digging into her brother's shoulders, gripping them fiercely. She looked him in the face. "I don't want outsiders to be here."

"You'll like them, Kate." Michael had on that earnest, worried look that Kate despised. "They're artists. Jane's a professional architect."

"It's not a matter of liking them, Michael. It's a matter of privacy . . . fuck . . . you could have . . . shit." She couldn't bring herself to feign civility right then. "You put me into this position, Michael. You can make excuses for me." And with that, Kate fled to the beach.

*   *   *

You could only get down to the beach one way, a steep flight of steps that slanted across the cliff's face. She took them fast and recklessly and was soon crunching across pebbles toward the waves, screaming at them.

She hadn't been in a real rage since she was a teenager. But this is where she had always come. She had come to pour her anger into the sea. She knew the sea could take it. Even her father had never seen her angry; she had always saved it for the Atlantic. And when she had moved to Montreal, seven hundred miles up the St. Lawrence, she had found herself empty of anger, unable to rouse it, despite her best efforts.

Now she was back. She was home, and it felt good to scream again. It wasn't just Michael's hired artists. It was Daniel and the house and everything. The futility of having come back here after not caring for so long.

When Kate returned to the house, Michael was clearing the remains of a lunch from the kitchen table. The others were unloading the van, producing computers and IKEA boxes and suitcases, piling them by the front door.

Michael looked at her, unsure of what to say.

"It's OK. I'm ready to be polite. Let's meet these artists."

"Kate, I thought . . ." Michael was tentative. He wanted to get the bad news over with all at once. "I thought they could have our old rooms. Yours, mine, Daniel's. And we could share Dad's old room?"

Kate stared at him and sighed. But all her anger had gone into the sea, and she shrugged. "Sure, whatever, Michael. That's fine. Just introduce me."

* * *

Jane, the architect, was a tall, powerful woman with a loud laugh and effortless charm. She would be responsible for modeling the house itself. She squeezed Kate's hand and kissed her on the cheek, saying, "It's such a pleasure to meet you at last, Kate. Michael's told us so much about you."

"Well, none of it's true," said Kate. She didn't even smile as she said it.

Toby was a photographer and texture artist. His business was the surface of things: the pattern of cracks in plaster, the roughness of stone, the grain in a tabletop. He was Jane's opposite, small and shy, with nervous eyes. He shook Kate's hand and gave a brief, uncertain smile.

And then there was Jamie. A classic nerd. Sideburns and thick glasses. He was a 3-D artist for a video-games company, and he would be modeling the house's contents, all the furniture and fixtures. He was a champion talker, and he started in on her at once. "It's good to meet you, Kate. An honor—an honor to be working for the children of Freddie Goldman. I'm sorry about his passing, by the way. He was a great man. A *great* man. Foundation revolutionized the industry. You can't write a software package like that on your own these days. You get teams of a hundred people working on them. Your dad was crazy. Crazy, am I right? I'll bet you two have been using it longer than anyone. Longer than *anyone*. I'll bet you and your brothers were the first beta testers. The very first. Still, he's probably just *Dad* to you, right? You probably took it for granted growing up. Thought he was nothing special. But he was. He *was*. No, he wasn't a household name. Not like a movie star or anything like that, but he was special. The top of his field. As I say, in the industry, he's a legend . . ."

Michael came to the rescue and suggested they all walk down to the beach to stretch their legs after the long drive.

* * *

That evening, they set up the computers in the basement. Three brand-new desktop Apple Macs with huge flat-panel monitors, and three metal IKEA computer desks for them to go on, plus two more laptops. Kate felt a giddy thrill pulling the desks from their oblong brown boxes and spreading the components on the floor. The prospect of transforming all these messy disparate pieces into one complete thing excited her. This power to reduce the number of objects in the universe, to simplify things. Again, that was her father talking. It depressed and comforted her to recognize him so clearly in herself.

When the computers were connected on the desks, the Ethernet cables strung between them, the software installed, and everything was ready to begin, Michael said, "Let's not start today. We'll wait until tomorrow. It's been a long trip. I'm sure we're all tired. Why don't you all just make yourselves at home and get to know the house a bit?"

* * *

That night, she slept beside Michael in their father's bed.

"How much have you told them?" she asked. "You haven't told them about Daniel, have you? You haven't!"

"Calm down. I just told them that he wanted to sell it and we wanted to keep it. That's all. Not of the rest of it."

"He's not crazy."

Michael was silent for a while, then rolled onto his side to face her. "You always understood him better than I did."

Kate felt like a child again, whispering secrets to her brother in the darkness. "We have to try to see it from his perspective. Dad was . . ."

"Overprotective," Michael conceded, "but a good and loving father."

"How many friends did we have here? How close were the nearest kids our age? How many times did he take us to that shitty homeschoolers' club in Digby?"

"Look around you. The ocean. The forest. It's a kid's paradise. A dreamland. Every day I spend in that shitty flat in Toronto I want to be back here. Don't you remember playing hide-and-seek here? The forts we built? The raft? I would love for my kids to grow up here. That can never happen now."

"But you never came back here."

There was no need to answer; it was just a statement. But Michael said, "Shit, Kate. I have a job. There's Sophie. And that's just it. I thought it would always be here, so . . ."

"Even when Dad was alive you didn't come here."

"OK. So I didn't come back. Neither did you."

"Neither did Daniel."

* * *

The next morning, they got to work. There was discussion over toast and coffee about how they should divide up the labor, what sort of standards they should use.

"Anything bigger than, say, two inches we'll model. Anything less than that we'll texture. So the doorframes will be 3-D, the wainscoting will just be texture."

It began with measurement. Jane supervised with a sketchbook, taking down dimensions of rooms, jotting quick floor plans. One room on each page, then a rough plan of the rooms in relation to one another for each floor. The others were down on their hands and knees with tape measures, shouting numbers to her.

There were more walls in the house than Kate ever would have believed. She had a cartoon idea of what a room was. Four walls, a floor, a ceiling. But now that she was forced to account for every wall, she realized that rooms weren't quite what they seemed. Alcoves and bay windows, jutting sections of wall impinging on other rooms, gentle curves. All of these complicated the matter, subdividing any given length of wall into dozens of shorter lengths.

This was the sort of thing her father ranted about: "From without, we think of the house as a solid block. But in fact it's mostly nothing, just empty space to occupy. As soon as we're inside this space, the house ceases to exist. It's just limits. Just environment. Just background. Just an arbitrary conceptual division—inside and outside. It lets us ignore the outside and thus provides a tidy and manageable space within which to organize the objects in our daily lives."

And that was how they structured things now, modeling the inside and outside of the house separately. Two separate worlds that you could move between simply by stepping through the doorway. It was simpler to do it that way and would take up less processor power.

* * *

Of the hired help, Kate liked Toby best. There was a constant need to protect herself from the other two, from Jane's easy intimacy and Jamie's siege of words. But Toby demanded nothing of her and seemed mildly terrified of conversation. Around Toby, she felt sure of herself.

It was one of Toby's jobs to photograph all the paintings. Kate helped him take them down and set them up on an easel in front of his tripod in the front hall, where the light was best. They worked in silence.

When the model was complete, the paintings—frames and all— would become two-dimensional, flattened against the wall, like wallpaper or paint.

* * *

The stairwell was difficult and time-consuming. There was no trick to it. Each step had to be a separate object, and the curve had to be exact so that it would emerge at the right place once it reached the second story. Jane set herself to the task with great patience while the others concentrated on furniture.

The World of Dew and Other Stories

Kate started with the study. It was in that study that Kate had first used Foundation at the age of ten, on her father's old Sun SPARCstation. That early beta testing that Jamie so romanticized. She had giggled with delight as she pulled geometric shapes out of thin air, shaped them as she pleased, glued them together or ripped them apart. She still remembered it as one of the happiest days of her life. Her father had been delighted at her enthusiasm, and that had made her all the more keen. She had fashioned crude ponies and houses and zeppelins, spinning them around and making them move with hints from her father about the controls and functionality of the program.

Michael had played around with it a bit, but he had been impatient and restless at that age. He didn't see the point. He lost interest. Daniel had wanted nothing to do with it. It had made him angry, even then, right from the beginning. He had been sixteen and had begun to rebel in a variety of ways, but Foundation seemed to particularly vex him. So Kate had been the beta tester, and her father grilled her for information that she was only too happy to provide. He had revised and rewritten according to her specifications, thrilled by her interest and talent.

The SPARCstation was long gone now, but Kate knew it had to be there in the model. She dashed off the coffee table, the couch, the bookshelves, the hi-fi cabinet and record player with careless skill, getting them out of the way. And then she set about re-creating the old computer from memory. Her style was rougher than Jamie's, but it was a far cry from the too-perfect geometry of the amateur. She had a better intuitive feel for Foundation than anyone else on the planet. It had been designed for her. For everyone else, it was a useful tool for making things, a virtual workbench plus an infinite supply of materials. But for her, and nobody else, it was an organ of pure expression.

By that evening, the SPARCstation stood there before her on the screen of her sleek laptop, looking boxy and dated. Old technology resurrected by new.

* * *

At dinner, she told them about the change she had made. "I built a phantom computer today. I want it to be in this model. I want to remember what this place was like when we were kids."

Michael agreed. He too remembered the Sun better than the PC that had replaced it. But then the disagreements began. "It's like that comfy brown couch in Daniel's old room," Michael said. "I think that should go back in the living room. That's how I remember it best."

Kate put down her fork. "Are you crazy? That was Daniel's couch. We can't just move it out of his room. We've had the green one in the living room forever."

"You said you wanted to remember this house as it was when we were kids. That couch was in the living room when we were kids. You don't remember doing somersaults onto it? Breaking your arm? It should be in the living room in the model."

"Michael, I can't have been older than six when we moved that couch. It's the new one that I remember. And, anyway, if we put the old one in the living room, then the new one can't exist at all. We can't very well put that one in Daniel's room; it was never there. With the new one in the living room and the old one in Daniel's room, we have the best of both worlds."

The others were visibly uncomfortable, but Toby would never have interrupted them, and Jane chose this moment to go to the bathroom. That left Jamie. "Yo, guys, guys, guys. You *can* have the best of both worlds. The best of *both* worlds. That's the beauty of computers. We'll just fork it. Make two versions."

There was a long silence as they all considered the implications of this, until at last Michael changed the subject. "Anyway, let's start on that dessert.

*　*　*

Kate had always dreamed of finding a secret cave down on the beach. Somewhere nobody else knew about, the entrance hidden by boulders. She would drag down one of the old rugs from the attic and spread it on the floor of her cave, maybe bring down some of the big cushions from the study or create a secret library down there from those books she found in the basement closet that everyone else had forgotten about, the ones with the magical names: *Ada, Lisp, Fortran, Cobol, Perl*— surely spell books.

Michael had decided to use a generic cliff generator to save time, just slapping on a randomized face of crinkly rock. But Kate went out with her laptop early one morning and copied the actual surface—broad strokes, but an honest copy, not just a random mess. She had spent countless hours walking up and down those cliffs looking for her cave. She knew them intimately, and it would matter if they weren't accurate.

That day was spent on ladders, modeling the roof and the chimneys. But that night, Kate stayed up late and opened up her virtual cliffs again. The entrance to the cave was narrow, with boulders and bushes concealing it from the beach. You would never notice it unless you knew what to look for. Kate textured the ground inside the cave with one of Toby's rug textures and pasted in a few chairs and a small bookcase from Jamie's ever-growing library of furniture. It was profoundly satisfying. As if all those hours of searching as a child had finally been rewarded. Her own secret cave that she could go to whenever she felt like it, even from her apartment in Outremont.

She added the cave to Michael's copy of the world too, smuggling it in with her version of the cliffs. It wouldn't really be secret if it only existed in her own private world. It was well hidden. He was unlikely to ever find it.

* * *

By the following Thursday, the virtual house was recognizable. Inside, you could visit all the rooms, open doors, and climb the stairs. All the main items of furniture were present. From the outside, you could walk all around it and see the walls, the windows, the door, the thatched roof. You could walk to the cliffs and look out over the Atlantic, stretching out to infinity.

Jamie told them that the physics engine, which governed how walking around worked, was licensed from a game called *Unreal*, which seemed a little on the nose to Kate.

The forest had been another point of contention. This time, Kate had been on the side of efficiency. "There are whole suites of software on the market for generating trees. We can just sprinkle a prefab Boreal Mix over the grounds and be done with it."

But while Kate had always been drawn to the cliffs and the beach, Michael's childhood had been spent building forts in that forest, battling elves and talking to the trees. There was one tree in particular that he insisted they model accurately. The rest could be generic, but this one had to be real. It was a grand old beech, hollow and split open at one side, allowing access to the nest of moss and bugs within. "You'll never get a tree like this out of a package."

"Trees are tricky," said Jamie. "But I'll do my best."

So Jamie spent the last day of his contract out at that tree with his laptop. In the afternoon, he commandeered Toby to cook up the bark and moss. Meanwhile, Jane was doing final checks and putting finishing touches on the building itself. That left Kate and Michael to work on whatever objects within the house they felt were important enough to include.

It felt arbitrary and pointless to Kate. The real house was full of old junk, and there was a potentially infinite number of things they could add, given enough time. The coat hangers in the closets, individual records and books, the contents of boxes in the attic that hadn't been opened in years. They would just have to let these things go and be satisfied with the big things, the important things. That tree, the cliffs, the cave.

"I could ask them to stay on," said Michael. He was making a stab at modeling a wicker fruit basket in the kitchen.

"No. I don't want them to be here when Daniel arrives."

"OK," said Michael. "And what about us?"

This was the question they had been avoiding all week. It had seemed like a question that would answer itself. But now a decision had to be made, and the answer was no clearer than when they had arrived.

"What do you think *he* wants?" asked Michael.

"I think he wants to see us," said Kate. "I think that's the real reason he sent those letters."

"Maybe he wants us to talk him out of doing it," said Michael.

"No. I wouldn't want to try. You know how stubborn he is."

"How stubborn he *was*," Michael corrected her. "He must have changed a lot. He must have."

"And yet he wants to burn it down. Like those origami models when we were kids. He hasn't changed. But we're his family. He loves us, and he wants to see us. Of that I'm sure."

"It's a funny way to show your love. No contact in ten years and then this."

"Yeah, it is funny." And then she began to laugh, a tired and hopeless laugh at the futility of it all.

Michael sighed. "Not funny like that, you idiot." But then he was laughing too.

*   *   *

"Michael, where did you find this?" Kate laughed. She stood in the study, clutching her morning coffee and staring at the old Sun SPARC-station.

Michael stopped dead as he entered the room. "I . . ." He looked at Kate, confused. "It must have been Jamie. That's incredible."

He sat down at the desk and ran his hands over the boxy monitor.

Kate was shaking her head. "No. Michael, something's weird. That's not some junk computer from eBay. That's *our* old computer. Look." She reached out and touched the peeling Decepticons sticker on the side of the enclosure. The sense of familiarity was so intense that it felt like vertigo, like she was lurching back in time to 1993.

"Nah . . . it can't be. We threw that computer out. I remember going to the recycling place in Digby. Kate, I remember going with Dad and watching them take it apart."

"It's our computer," said Kate. She shoved her hip against Michael's, and he slid over to share the chair. "It's ours."

"It can't be," Michael said again. He was chuckling to himself. "Jamie, you maniac. Where did you find this?"

Kate reached behind the enclosure and flicked the power switch. The fans whirred into life, and the screen lit up.

"No! It still works? These things are collectors' items. He must have paid a fortune."

"It's *our* SPARCstation, Michael," Kate said. Her voice was shaky now. The blue Sun logo appeared on the screen, and then the folders and windows of Solaris OS. With trembling hands, Kate navigated to the Foundation (Beta) folder. There it was. Her old folder, labeled *KAte* with a capital *A*. And inside were all her creations.

* * *

She spent all day playing with her old models, the ponies and houses and zeppelins, playing and replaying her old animations. Michael still insisted that Jamie must have found the thing on eBay—that some Foundation fanboy must have lovingly preserved their father's computer for all these years and that Jamie had tracked it down. But Kate could tell he didn't believe what he was saying. He was shaken and angry, the way he always got when he didn't understand something.

It was dark by the time Kate got up from the computer to pee. Her bladder and eyes ached. The light had faded hours earlier, and she had been so engrossed that she had not turned on any of the lights in the study. She rushed to the downstairs bathroom and sighed with relief. As a child, she had once become so obsessed with the details of one of her models that she had wet herself while sitting at the computer. It was after that that her father had started to impose time limits on her.

As she was washing her hands, a shout from the living room startled her. She rushed in with dripping hands to see Michael staring at the old brown couch, the one that had been in Daniel's room ever since his thirteenth birthday.

"Michael," Kate said, "we discussed this." But even as she said it, she knew something was wrong.

"Kate," Michael said softly, "go up to Daniel's room."

Kate went. And there it was. The same couch, in Daniel's room. The same one.

* * *

They sat at the kitchen table, drinking the last of the beer.

"Maybe he'll change his mind if he knows." Michael was beginning to mumble, as he did when he was drunk or tired.

"If he knows what? If he knows that there are two couches that look the same? If he knows there's an old computer in the office?"

"You know what I mean."

"I do. But think about explaining it to him. To anyone. Imagine how that conversation would go."

"Are we crazy?"

"Yeah, maybe," Kate laughed. "It's not something that can *actually* happen. So I guess we must be."

"We've been staring at that fucking model for too long. Maybe we should just delete it and get the fuck out of here. Leave it to Daniel to burn down."

Kate smiled. Michael swore when he was drunk. But Kate felt fine. She felt as though she could accept anything without questioning it. "We'll figure it out in the morning," she said.

*　*　*

He must have arrived during the night. Kate had risen at sunrise to swim in the sea. When she got back to the house, there he was, at the breakfast table, helping himself to bacon and eggs.

"Hi, Kate," he said, as if there was nothing unusual about his being there. "You want some? I made lots."

Kate just stared for a bit in disbelief. She had been fourteen when she had last seen him. He had left, furious and determined, striking out on his own with his army-surplus backpack and long hair. He had left Michael and Kate in tears, but their father had remained calm.

"He'll be back," he had assured them. "It's just a phase. Needs to individuate himself. Needs to become his own person, distinct from his family. We're all individuals, after all. Daniel just needs to explore that."

But Daniel didn't come back. Weeks passed, and they had no word, no calls, no postcards. Her father remained unfazed. "He needs time," he had assured them. "He'll be back. He loves us. Never doubt that."

A year later, they received a postcard. A careless scrawl: "I just wanted to let you all know I'm doing fine." That was it. No signature. No return address. The postcard was from Glasgow, but the stamp and postmark were Italian.

"There you go," her father had said, smiling. "He's doing fine. He just needs time."

As if the last twelve months of killing anxiety hadn't happened.

At some point, Kate stopped thinking about him. He was something of their past, like their mother, like a beloved childhood cartoon that no longer aired. It wasn't until Kate left for university in Australia that she began to think about him again. It was as if she was more likely to meet him in Adelaide than back home. This was a foreign place, and he was somewhere foreign. She began to see people who looked like him on the street. Once, she chased a man with the same hair, the same backpack, down the street for half a block. A baffled stranger.

And now here he was, sitting at the breakfast table, offering her bacon and eggs. She sat down at the table with him and let him scrape some eggs and bacon from the pan onto a plate. She munched, as nonchalant as him.

"So you got my letter, I take it?" he asked. "That's why you're here, right?"

"Yes, Michael and I both got your letters." Her own voice sounded alien and overformal.

"I'm glad you're having a good time." He nodded to the empty beer cans on the counter. "I thought it was only fair to let you say goodbye. Been having a bit of a party?"

"Only fair. Yes, only fair," said Kate, not looking at him now, speaking quickly, pushing her eggs around her plate. "Maybe it would have been only fair to talk about what you were going to do with the house with me and Michael? Don't you think that would have been the fair thing to do? It's ours too."

"No it isn't. Dad left it to me." Daniel shrugged. "Who knows why?"

"Why *did* he leave it to you? Have you ever thought about that? Michael and I have been wondering that ever since the funeral. Why do *you* think he left it to you?" Kate couldn't believe how quickly they had reverted to the old quarrels of childhood. All those years apart, and already they were bickering.

"I know what you want me to say." Daniel grinned. "So that I'd always have a place to come home to. Right? But I think you're wrong. I think Dad would have approved."

"Approved?" Kate stared in disbelief. "You're crazy. You're a lunatic, Daniel. And you meant it literally, didn't you? What you said in the letter. You're not just going to have it knocked down. You're actually going to burn it."

"You bet," said Daniel with a smile. "It'll be glorious. Like bonfire night. I haven't had a real Guy Fawkes night since I left Britain. I hope you're planning to stick around for it. We can make it a real family thing. The three of us together again at last."

"No, Daniel. We're not going to *stick around*. As soon as we're finished with the model, we're leaving. We don't want anything to do with you."

"Model?" said Daniel, knitting his eyebrows. "I had wondered about those computers in the basement."

"Yes. We're saving this place and creating a testament to Dad all at once."

"Don't tell me. In Foundation, right?" Daniel threw his head back and gave a laugh, loud and hearty. "I should have known."

"Right," said Kate, determined to hold her ground. The whole project seemed silly and overdramatic now that she was telling it to Daniel. An extravagant and meaningless gesture on par with Daniel's own plan for the place.

"It's important to *us*, Daniel. Even if it means nothing to you, this place is important to us. And doing this will at least save something. And listen—I know this is going to sound crazy, but . . ."

"You fucking asshole." Michael was standing at the kitchen door in his bathrobe. He had a grin on his face and tears in his eyes.

*   *   *

They began by soaking the lengths of rag in kerosene from buckets, laying them out on a fire-resistant tarp. The gas mains had been shut off, the electricity and water disconnected, the pipes drained. The pump at the old well was working, and there were hoses and extinguishers on hand. Daniel had chopped down the closest trees with a chainsaw and dragged them out of the way with his truck. He had already burned away most of the grass around the house, and the sprinklers had been on all night, soaking the ground until it was soft and marshy.

They pulled the stinking lengths of rag through the house. Up the stairs, wound them around pillars. Kate's hands shook as she laid out the rags, not quite believing what she was doing, what she had agreed to. It would burn so easily, with so much wood and the thatched roof. It was the thought of that roof going up in flames that made her cry.

"The new one will be smaller, made of stone with a slate roof," Daniel said. "*My* kids are going to have more of a challenge."

But when it was done, when she sat on the hill, with Daniel on her right, Michael on her left, it felt fine. Just fine. The cliffs would still be there once it was gone, the forest, the sea. All that would remain. The house was just a thing, after all. And she could create things just by thinking about it. There—that patch of sky framed between the branches of that tree, the shape of India. That was a thing. Same as the house was. Just space enclosed by wood. Just a thing, just nothing.

"Ready?" said Daniel.

"No," said Michael. "I'm never going to be ready. It's not too late to change your mind, Daniel."

"Yes it is," said Kate, putting her arms around her brothers' shoulders and giving them both a rough hug. "We're ready."

When it was all over, Kate went down to the beach to find her cave.

Keeping It Real

GINNIE IS A JAGGYPUNK WITH BIG, ABRASIVE PIXELS AND AN attitude to match. She's one of my best mates, and she's such fun that I give her unrestricted access. She can drop in on me whenever she likes. Doesn't even have to knock. She just pops into existence and makes life interesting. That's how she comes now, grinning and badly rendered, sticking out like a sore dick among the warrior nymphs and grimwood trees of Darkhart Forest.

My party and I are preparing to attack a dryad fortress when she arrives. We're huddled around a campfire, speaking in hushed tones about siege magic and weapons loadouts. Ginnie's appearance utterly destroys the atmosphere.

"Who the fuck let her in here?" screams Galhan the Alchemist. "Is she with you, Mordrak? We *told you* to go private when we began."

I shrug but can't suppress a bit of a grin. A few seconds ago, I had been totally into the adventure—honestly I had!—but whenever Ginnie arrives, I stop caring. Ginnie's always onto something good. Nothing's important when she's around, but everything's worth doing.

"Galhan's right," says Lauriella the Mage in her ultrareasonable voice. "We can't keep playing like this. If this keeps happening, we'll have to report you to GigaGuild, and nobody wants to do that."

"Fuck this shit," observes Ginnie, looking around at the primeval forest with undisguised contempt. "Let's go, Olly. I've got something to show you. Or should I say *Mordrak*?" She laughs, just to be a douche, but Ginne's laughter is contagious, and I can't say no.

"Listen, I'm really sorry, Galhan. Can we pause for a bit? Or you can go on without me. I'll catch up later. Tell the others I'm laying up at the Way's End Inn with a case of swamppox."

Lauriella summons burst-lightning to her fingertips and unleashes it at Ginnie in searing arcs of deadly energy. Not party to the opt-in physics of our current world, Ginnie just ignores it.

"Fuck you, Mordrak," says Galhan. "I'll get the GM to fucking delete your character."

"I'm sorry," I say, almost sincere. Ginnie gives Galhan the finger, and then we're out of there. The respectful thing to do would have been to walk a little way until we were out of Galhan's sight. There were enough trees around that this would only have taken a few seconds. But Ginnie is a jaggypunk, and she's having none of it. We zap out of there like the inconsiderate shits that we are, violently destroying any suspension of disbelief that remained.

I glom on to Ginnie's location and find myself in her apartment. She claims not to give a shit about it, but I secretly suspect she spends a lot of time sourcing her blurry furniture and getting her glitchy, jaggy decor just wrong.

"This had better be good, Ginnie," I say with a smile on my face. "Galhan can be a real dick when he wants to be."

"So go find another bunch of children to play with."

"Shut up! It's good fun. And if they start bad-mouthing me, I could lose my membership in GigaGuild."

"So go get a membership somewhere else. There are a million. I mean *literally* a million."

Ginnie sends me an attachment that pops up in my public interface. It's a list of the first million active gaming guilds registered on OmniSource. I return fire with the current edition of *The GameTrash Top 100 Guilds Guide*, which lists GigaGuild at a respectable number three, behind only the Gygax Brotherhood and the GamerGate Goon Crew.

"You want me to join GamerGate? Is that what you want? I'll do it, just to piss you off."

"Come on—this'll be worth it," she says. "Trust me."

Something new pops up in my 'face. It's a philter, and it's rigged to affect some pretty basic stuff about my perception.

"What's that?"

"You'll see," says Ginnie. "Just accept it."

"I'm not just going to accept it. Your philters always turn out to be either boring or painful."

Ginnie looks wounded. Or at least I imagine she does. It's hard to say with jaggypunks. "What, you didn't like MegaGravity SuperParty?"

"It gave me the worst headache I've ever had."

"Well, anyway, I didn't code this one. Just take a look at the meta. Only lasts half an hour and doesn't even cross any thresholds."

I pull up the metainfo for the philter, and I see that Ginnie is telling the truth. It's titled Infinite Emptiness, and it's authored by someone named Henry. I have no idea who Henry is, but he must be pretty old to have a username like that. Kids these days are born with 256 random characters appended to their usernames, just to guarantee uniqueness.

"Come on, don't be a crashbuggler. Just take it."

With a deep breath, I accept the philter and wait for it to fuck with me.

Nothing happens.

"Slow building. Come on. Let's check out the Latest while we wait."

The Latest is our favourite underground aggregation service. We discovered it through NoveltyAddict, which used to be our favorite underground aggregation service. The Latest describes itself as "The Latest and Greatest for Creatives & People Who Care," a tagline that Ginnie insists is ironic somehow.

We zap into the Latest Lobby and see ten portals before us, leading to the ten best new worlds, according to whatever esoteric criteria the AI behind the Latest uses to generate its rankings. If you look at each portal for long enough, it blasts you with streams of information until you get the idea. There's a hippie paradise called New Eden, some sort of cutting-edge distributed education center, a couple of music venues and art spaces, and a broadcasting platform called NowSound. But Ginnie and I decide to check out SkyWorldOne.

There's a dress code, so we're barred entry until we come up with a skin "that looks like it could reasonably fly." Ginnie has one ready. She becomes some sort of cyborg birdman with a bionic eye and rocket engine—jaggy, of course. I duck into Foundation for a few minutes to cobble together an old-timey Leonardo da Vinci–esque flying machine.

And then we're in SkyWorldOne, plummeting toward the ground. There's a blinking message in my 'face, asking me if I want to opt in to the world's physics. I tell it yes. And then I can fly, slowly and clumsily. I watch Ginnie hit the ground, hard. She goes from terminal velocity to zero in a span of zero seconds—then ignites her rocket boosters, and she's flying with me.

There's some sort of leveling mechanic built into this world, so loyal users and major contributors get to fly faster and more nimbly. As noobs, we plod through the air while elite users swoop and dive around us. We're flying through a user-generated castle in the clouds when a zeppelin full of sky pirates attacks. There's a combat mechanic, so corpses are soon dropping out of the sky.

"Look at that," says Ginnie. "That's a perfect example."

"Example of what?"

"A flying castle is under attack by sky pirates, and we don't give a shit, right?"

"What do you mean?"

"Like, it's no big deal. Just a bunch of kids playing around. Nothing *important* can happen anymore." We swoop through a series of arches into an aviary where griffins are nesting.

"What are you getting at, Ginnie? You're not going all philosophical on me, are you?"

"It's just a bunch of desperate nerds clambering over each other for cultural capital. They want so badly to be seen, to be heard, to be liked. They want to be seen to be having fun so badly that they don't even know what it means to have fun anymore."

"Ginnie, seriously. You're not making sense."

"Listen to me. What's the point of being a jaggypunk?"

I sigh. "You tell me. You're the jaggy."

"It's a rejection of all that shit. It's a rejection of trying to keep up with the next big thing. It's a rejection of dumb standards of beauty."

At this point, the philter starts to kick in. It begins by draining all the color from the world. Bit by bit, the clouds and the sky and the griffins and gyrocopters and rocket men and sky pirates drift toward grayscale.

"Can you feel it?" says Ginnie. "It's about rejecting all this shit and just being yourself."

Once all the world is composed of grays instead of colors, the shades begin to diminish. Objects that are fairly close in color become indistinguishable from one another. I look at my own hand, and it's a solid plane of a single shade, a gray silhouette of a hand.

"It's about dealing with yourself." Ginnie is still talking. "Because, at the end of the day, that's all you've got."

My body is indistinguishable from the surroundings now. It doesn't matter where we are, because everything looks the same. And as all distinctions evaporate, I begin to see what Ginnie's going on about. This undifferentiated grayness is just as real as SkyWorldOne or my RPG or Ginnie's house.

My vision drops to nil, and all I see is gray wherever I turn. And I feel as though I'm a part of something much larger than myself, this vast gray absence.

I can't hear Ginnie anymore. I can't hear anything. I no longer have a skin. My flying machine is gone. I'm nothing but a pure organ of perception, tiny and insignificant.

It's slightly cold.

I wait like that, doing nothing, because there's nothing to do. How could there possibly be anything to do? I don't have a body anymore. I can't communicate or play or fly or walk around. I wait and wait, just *experiencing*.

At long last, after what seems like an age, the world begins to come back into focus. I know from the metainfo on the philter that it can't have been more than half an hour, but it feels as though I was gone for an hour, a week, a lifetime. I was in a place where time didn't exist.

I look around and find myself on the ground. The ground in Sky-WorldOne is not somewhere you want to be. It's a basic pattern, repeated ad infinitum in all directions. Nobody put much thought or work into this ground. All the action is above. There's no sign of Ginnie, so I drop a message into her head.

The message just bounces, which is when I begin to worry. Ginnie is always open to communication from me. We allow each other in, answer each other's calls, and drop whatever we're doing to have fun and talk shit. My messages to her have never bounced, and yet they're bouncing now, as if she's unfriended me or dropped out of the universe altogether.

I zap into my own bedroom and lie down, a little shaken. Where the hell is Ginnie?

I'm woken from a doze by a ping from Garth. "Yo, buddy. You down for BlastMaster tonight? The whole crew's gonna be there."

"What about Ginnie?" I ping back. "You seen her around?"

"No, man. She's not responding. Weird."

"Sure. Whatevs. I'll come."

*　*　*

It's months later now. I'm riding a surfboard down a river of lava in PurgatoryVVV. I'm at an art show in an infinite, procedurally generated cathedral cooked up by some deranged goths. I'm floating naked on a warm lake while stars go supernova overhead. And I know none of it is real.

I haven't heard from Ginnie since that day when everything went gray, but I know she's out there—*experiencing*.

I know she's out there, dealing with the only thing that's real.

I know she's out there, free of all the bullshit, all the clamoring for attention, all the manipulation and hype and masturbatory backslapping that we call the universe.

I know she's out there, being punk as fuck and keeping it real so that we don't have to.

And even though I miss her, that somehow makes life bearable.

An Oral History of the City Beneath

I WASN'T THE ONE WHO FIRST DISCOVERED THE CITY Beneath, despite what the Wiki says. That honor goes to Johnny Grayson, who fell through the floor of a gun emplacement while exploring the abandoned naval base up at Government Point. He broke his foot in the fall, but he was a tough little bastard. Managed to scramble out. Ought to have gone straight to the hospital, but he came to me instead, giddy with excitement and delirious with pain in his torn leather jacket.

Of course, I didn't believe him at first. Assumed he was trying to play a trick on me or possibly get into my pants. But I had always had a bit of a crush on Johnny Grayson, and his tricks were usually fun. So I sneaked out of the house and went with him. Helped him hobble all the way back to Government Point. He was in pretty rough shape and ended up leaning on me as he hopped along, but he refused to turn back.

"You have to see this. Trust me."

And I kinda did.

We climbed Magazine Hill, peeled back the sheet of chain link, and climbed into the concrete casemate that had once housed artillery pieces. Kids from the school came here sometimes to smoke and drink and make out. The ground was littered with bottles and butts. I had come here once or twice, back when I dated Andy Cunningham, but I hadn't been in years.

Johnny used his phone in flashlight mode. He led us down a tunnel and into the magazine itself, a monstrous room where they used to keep the shells for the guns. It was empty and echoing now, just a dusty cavity deep in the hill.

Johnny sat against the wall and winced as he regained his breath. He was in serious pain. But now that he had come this far, he wasn't about to turn back. Something about the place made me think it must be something morbid. A dead body, perhaps, or a stash of nuclear material. I loved that shit.

In the back corner of the room was a steel closet, barely bigger than an outhouse. Probably used to contain a Shop-Vac and mop. Johnny led me over to it and pointed his phone at the floor. There was nothing there but a jagged hole where the concrete had given way.

"Careful," he said. "This is how I fucked up my leg."

"How far down does it go?"

"Not far. But it's rubble at the bottom. I landed wrong. If you're careful . . ."

I peered down through the hole and saw a heap of rock and iron bulging in the dark. "What's down there?"

He just smiled.

If I chickened out now, I'd never live it down. So I swung my legs over the edge and lowered myself into the pit. Johnny was right. Even with my short legs, I could almost touch the pile of rubble beneath. The drop was only a few inches.

I helped Johnny down after me, supporting him at the waist, like a rugby player lifting a teammate for a throw-in. He was heavier than I expected, so I didn't let him down as gently as I should have. He swore and held his breath at the pain in his ankle, but he was so excited he wasn't even mad.

"Come on," he said.

We crept along a narrow tunnel with a low ceiling. Then we descended a set of stairs. It was a long stairway. With the adrenaline and nerves, it was hard to tell how long it took us. Johnny went slow with his fucked-up foot, but we now know it was more than five hundred stairs. When we reached the bottom, Johnny stopped and rested again. He looked a funny color in the cell-phone light, but that glint of excitement returned to his eyes.

"Look." He handed me the phone and gestured for me to shine it over the edge. It took a moment for me to realize it, but it became clear we were standing on a balcony that jutted from a wall of rock. We were in some sort of chamber. A cave. It stretched as far as the light would go in every direction, with countless side passages, chasms, and tubes leading off into shadow. It was by far the biggest enclosed space I had ever been in. Below us was nothing but darkness, a bottomless abyss.

But the cave was not a cave. Or rather, that's not all it was. The cave contained a city. It was vast and intricate, cut from the rock, like a thousand Petras stacked on top of one another. The city had infested every square inch of the cave, a metropolis of steeples, domes, amphitheaters—all made from that soft limestone, all bearing alien carvings.

I stood for a long time, shining the light down at the city that sprawled in the darkness. It was unimaginable that this place existed beneath our little town. What civilization had built it? How long had it lain here, unnoticed?

I turned to Johnny. The battery on his phone was almost dead, and I didn't want to get trapped down here in the dark. I turned to him with wonder in my eyes and a grin on my face.

I turned to him. But he was gone.

* * *

Winders: These spooks slither through the air like eels through water. They're roughly the size of pool noodles. They glow green, but occasionally I'll see a ripple of blue go through one. They tend to move through the air in tight spirals. They make a very low moaning sound. They're the most numerous of all the spooks I've seen down here, outnumbering Howlers (the next most common) by two to one. They're usually floating out near the middle of the chamber, above the Abyss, and they seem to avoid getting too close to bridges, so I couldn't approach them even if I wanted to. This one is about as close as I've ever gotten. (linkto: Winder14-7.mov)

* * *

So the search parties were the first to explore, and I went with them, leading the lads from Ground Search and Rescue into the City Beneath. I led them into the underground, showed them exactly where he had disappeared. They brought real flashlights and flares and ropes. There wasn't much caving around these parts. They usually went looking for folks lost in the woods. But they were mostly fishermen, so they knew their knots. We climbed down the stairways and across stone arch bridges. They weren't natural. They had been *made*. They had railings and everything.

We poked our flashlights into vast cathedrals of carved stone and hollered Johnny's name. It echoed through the dark of the City Beneath. We went down and down, but we never found the bottom of the city. You could lean over a balcony and shine your light down and see nothing but darkness beneath, nothing but the Abyss. And then, as your eyes adjusted, out of the darkness would loom buildings and arches and bridges.

If he had fallen . . . but no, that didn't make sense. He would have been caught on a ledge or another balcony directly beneath the one where we had stood. Either his body had been moved or he had not fallen—simply vanished.

We were down there for hours with our flashlights and flares and ropes. And on that night, we saw our first ghosts.

It was Howlers and Winders at first, glowing faintly in the gloom of the caverns. We thought their voices were the sounds of wind howling through the rock crevices. But then we saw them.

It's hard to explain what it was like, seeing those first few. You have to imagine a time before FlashCapture, before the badges and achievements and media coverage. Before they disappeared.

It's funny to think back on it, but it was terrifying. We ran from the cave, me and those burly fisherman, scared out of our wits. But we went back with guns and baseball bats. The ghosts were still there. Howlers and Winders and Creepers and Bulbs. They didn't hurt us, of course, but we worried that they might.

And we didn't find Johnny Grayson.

* * *

Howlers: These guys are the scariest of the spooks down here. They appear literally out of nowhere, growing rapidly from a single point and streaking diagonally upward through the air, then vanishing. At their fattest, they're maybe three feet wide. When they appear, they let out a howl not unlike that of a wolf—or maybe a pack of wolves, because I'm pretty sure there are a couple of different pitches in there. Have a listen, and let me know what you think in the comments. (linkto: Howler27-7.mov)

* * *

I started my blog in the summer of '09. I had finished school, gone to college, come back, and grown bored of small-town life. I knew I should be in the city looking for a career, a lover, a life that Yarmouth couldn't offer. But the City Beneath kept me there. It lay in the darkness, waiting for me.

They had closed it off, of course. The feds had come in and put up warning signs around the gun emplacement, repaired the fences, added CCTV cameras. Then everyone forgot about it.

The kids from the local high school didn't go there to drink anymore. It was a new crop of adolescents by then. My generation had wanted dank caves that protected us from the world. These kids wanted to drink in the midst of forests or on the edge of cliffs overlooking the ocean. Minecraft childhoods had given these kids a yearning for scenery and fresh air.

I dithered for two years before I went. Two years of dull jobs and no social life to speak of. Two years of living in my old bedroom in my parents' house. For two years, I dreamed about going. And then, one night, I went.

The cameras and fences were still up, but I knew another way in. There was an old escape tunnel that led from the main system out into the woods behind the base. It hadn't been touched since the war, and was still full of rust and rubble. I tore open the chain link, switched on my flashlight, made my way to the magazine, and descended.

That was the beginning of my blog.

These days, I would have livestreamed the whole thing, of course, but you didn't get reception down there back then. So I just recorded video on my phone and posted it to a basic WordPress page. I posted videos of the ghosts, walk-throughs of the cathedrals, panoramas from the stone arches. I posted theories about who had built this place and why and what had happened to them.

Those early posts are a little embarrassing. You can still go back and read them. I insisted they archive everything back when FlashCapture took over. Now I wish I hadn't. I sounded nuts, like one of those conspiracy peddlers talking about aliens visiting earth. Although now that I think about it, nobody has ever offered a better explanation than that. Maybe it was aliens after all.

Even in those days, nobody read blogs. Everyone wanted live-streams, real-time interaction with dumbass influencers doing stupid shit. Even if I had had Wi-Fi, I wouldn't have been able to give them any of that. I was slow, cautious, and meticulous. I never approached a ghost. I always watched them from a distance as they twisted and flowed through the dark, their translucent bodies glowing like the hands of a radium watch. I watched and cataloged their kinds. And that was the start of the SpookSpotter series.

* * *

Bulbs: These dudes just kinda bob in the air, like fishing buoys. They have the dimmest glow of any of the spooks down here, but they cluster into groups of ten or twelve. Each one is pretty big, about the size of one of those inflatable fitness balls. They're quite beautiful, bobbing gently in the darkness. Sometimes, I get the impression that they're breathing. What do you think? (linkto: BulbColony16-8.mov)

* * *

Occasionally, I'd bring a friend or a date with me, but no one wanted to go down there more than once. Everyone I invited down there freaked the fuck out as soon as they saw the ghosts and swore they were never coming back.

Ever since Johnny Grayson had disappeared, the locals treated the City Beneath like some sort of curse on the town. They were reluctant to even acknowledge its existence, and when they did, they lowered their voices, as if it might hear them talking. It had somehow become a source of civic shame, a story to scare children with.

I liked the ghosts. I found their gentle glow calming. Nothing in my life really seemed to matter within the context of that dead city. If I had disappeared, like Johnny Grayson, I don't think I would have minded.

The first Spookheads found me through my blog. They were the kind of cranks who went to UFO conferences and believed in chemtrails, but they were willing to pay for a tour. So I met them at the airport, drove them the four hours from the airport to Yarmouth, and took them down with me.

It was probably a stupid thing to do. I didn't have a business license or any insurance. If one of them had slipped and fallen into the Abyss, I would have been fucked. But those first tours were a blast. The tourists were thrilled with what they saw, and I was proud to show them. I felt a certain amount of ownership over the City Beneath and its ghosts.

The tourists set up tripods and shot video. And I felt like a proud parent or a hipster who can get into the hottest after-parties. The only people I was impressing were paranoid conspiracy theorists with wild hair, but that was good enough for me.

I was working at Hamelin's at the time, slinging coffee in the morning and beer in the evening. But in my free time, I was building a small business. I was stupid, but I knew I should take some basic safety precautions. So I borrowed my granddad's old pickup truck and drove out to the entrance with cleaning supplies and tools and hardware. I cleaned up the worst of the broken glass and bolted a stepladder to the edge of the hole that led down to the stairs that led down to the City Beneath. I put up a railing and put fluorescent yellow caution tape around the edge of the hole. I used a crowbar to lever out some of the rubble and a wheelbarrow to cart it out of the way.

I began to advertise without really advertising. I added a page to my blog about booking a tour without actually using the word *booking* or mentioning any prices. I started commenting on ghost-hunting and conspiracy blogs. I got the names of message boards and YouTube channels from my clients. I friended them on Facebook and Instagram and liked their posts. I thanked them for coming in the comments and told them to tell their friends and linked to my blog. I got cards printed up and handed them out to all the tourists. They said, "Visit the City Beneath—Ghost Watching Expeditions & Tours."

In Yarmouth itself, I kept quiet. Business was growing, and I didn't want anyone muscling in on my racket. Most of the locals wouldn't go anywhere near the place where Johnny Grayson had disappeared, but I bet Lucas Grishwell or Marian Outhouse would be all over it if they knew there was money to be made.

Efrim Michaels was the first real influencer I took down with me. He said he was a freelance journalist, which anyone could say, but you could tell he was serious. He had a nice camera and a well-used notebook, and he knew how to take photographs and video in the dark. He also got me to sign waivers to be in the photos and asked if he could publish my contact information wherever he sold the article. Stupidly, I said yes. A month later, it was a cover feature in Atlas Obscura. From there, it got picked up by Gawker and Vice, and then it was featured on some Lonely Planet viral property.

Back in '12, I was doing around a tour a month and making a bit of pocket money on Saturday evenings. By '13, I had quit my job at Hamelin's and was booking Tuesday mornings six months out.

By now, it had hit the local news. They're always the last to know, even when news is happening right in their own backyard, but you couldn't ignore the uptick in tourism. The old shuttered Colony Hotel reopened, and two new shuttle services started doing airport runs.

I bumped my prices and started offering new tiers of service. For $600, you could get a basic ghost-spotting tour. For $2,000, you could spend the night in the structure that I had dubbed the Grand Cathedral. For $5,000, you could join me as I went into an unexplored area.

I'd been steadily exploring and mapping for years by that point. With every new expedition, I saw new ghosts. I had cataloged hundreds by now. There were Drifters and Screamers and Wanderers and Bloaters and Statues and Hairies. They each had quite distinct behaviors and appearances. For example, Statues stayed perfectly still until you got close, and then they zipped away with surprising speed, coming to an abrupt stop in a new location. Hairies crackled with thin filaments of electricity—or something similar—that looked like little hairs. They seemed to be attracted to other ghosts, moving toward them until the crackling hairs touched. Wanderers moved fairly quickly, but

The World of Dew and Other Stories

seemingly randomly, zigzagging through the void like bags blown in the wind, beautiful and mindless.

At first, my competitors were local amateurs who didn't have a clue. Tourists could tell they were scared, even as they pretended to know all about the ghosts and the City Beneath. I giggled as I read their Yelp reviews.

"Didn't seem confident. Not at all knowledgeable. I wasn't even sure we were safe . . . and I don't think he was sure either." Two stars.

Meanwhile, my clients loved my confidence and ease. I felt more at home down there than I did on the surface. Sometimes, I would bring my camping stuff on a multiday spelunking expedition into the lower levels. The city went on and on. It seemed to have no bottom and an infinite number of side passages. Every trip revealed a new chamber in the rock full of carved buildings and bas-relief and ghosts.

Where locals failed, the big companies did no better. They tried to professionalize it, but that brought the government down on them. The province sent inspectors to make sure everything was safe—and of course nothing was. Insurance premiums were through the roof. I seemed to get grandfathered in. In fact, the inspectors hired me to take them down there, as if I was just a part of the fabric of the place. While the inspectors were marking big red x's on their forms, I was booking my next tour group.

* * *

And then it happened. Dan was a young app developer from Detroit. His company only had seven employees at the time. That company was FlashCapture.

I was living in the City Beneath full-time by then. I had taken over one of the smaller side chambers, furnished it with comfy chairs and a composting toilet, a cot, and a generator. There was a subterranean river down there that spilled over a carved lip of rock to a sloped shelf near my front door. That's where I bathed. I had rigged up a series of Wi-Fi boosters and managed to get spotty reception down there. I only came to the surface to meet clients and stock up on food.

Dan had paid the big bucks for a private expedition into an unexplored section. As we started out, I could already tell he was smitten.

He was nervous, like everyone on their first trip down, but he loved every moment of it. The seeds of the idea were already planted on that first trip. Maybe he'd already had a rough idea before he went down. He said he had read my blogs. But back then, FlashCapture was just working on a generic pattern-recognition neural net that could detect common objects in photographs—faces, cars, trees, stuff like that.

On that trip, we spotted a new ghost. My first Bubbler. And I blogged about it that night. Meanwhile, Dan rented a long-term Airbnb in Yarmouth and booked every available tour for the next month.

We started dating. It was mostly my idea. I joked that he was spending so much time in the City Beneath that he should give up his Airbnb and move down there with me. So he did. But he wasn't that interested in me, and—truth be told—I wasn't that interested in him. We were both in love with the City Beneath and its ghosts.

After a month of expeditions and hundreds of hours of video, he went back to Detroit. But every few weeks, he would bring a team back to Yarmouth to test their latest build.

A year later, the first version of FlashCapture was released. It was a simple concept. All you had to do was use the app to take a picture of a ghost. The app would recognize the type and catalog it for you. You got more points for taking pictures of rarer ghosts. You got an Achievement for spotting one of every kind within a particular area. There was a list of ghosts you hadn't snapped yet, with their shapes in silhouette with big question marks over them, obscuring the detail. When you found one, you would take a picture, and the question mark would disappear, color and detail would bloom, and a description would appear, listing everything we knew about the ghost. The descriptions were based on my descriptions from my blog, lightly edited by some intern at Flash-Capture. Dan paid me in stock.

I must admit, I didn't think much of it when I first tried it out. It was silly and fun but didn't seem like it would change anything.

I was wrong, of course.

* * *

Corporations that had failed before now had tech money behind them. They began running slick professional tours, and this time the

The World of Dew and Other Stories

government helped them do it. They renovated the entrance to the City Beneath and excavated a service ramp so they could bring down supplies. They installed handrails on the bridges that spanned the Abyss using some kind of clamping technology that wouldn't harm the structure. You could read all about it on the "Preserving the City Beneath" page of their website.

Spookheads flocked to the town from all over the world. It was Silicon Valley types at first, then the type of people who attended Burning Man. One summer, it was a craze among Koreans, and they started running direct flights form Seoul to Yarmouth's tiny airport. The whole town transformed itself in an effort to cash in. Every other shop on Main Street turned into a gift shop selling plushie Bulbs or novelty underwear that said, "Explore the City Beneath!" The local museum added a wing dedicated to it. The coffee shops were full of Spookheads, bragging about having unlocked every ghost in Level 7 or discovering new ghosts or venturing into unexplored areas.

I was still living down there, but I had to move my home twice as my former locations became overrun by Spookheads. Each time, I moved it farther down into the cave, farther along obscure side passages. I put up official Keep Out signs with the FlashCapture logo, but still I would get visitors from time to time, Spookheads who thought it was edgy to ignore the signs and explore forbidden areas.

By that point, I was hardly running any tours myself. The FlashCapture stock that Dan had given me was worth millions, and there were plenty of young, talented, friendly guides who were more than happy to work for barely above minimum wage. At FlashCapture's request, I would occasionally give a tour to a visiting dignitary or VIP, but I mostly kept to myself, living a solitary life among the ghosts.

Spookheads began to post about sightings of me, as if I were one of the ghosts myself. As you know, I became a part of the mythology of the place. And then someone at FlashCapture—I suspect Dan, but I'll never know for sure—added me to the app. You could get a special Achievement if you captured a photograph of "the Hermit of the City Beneath." When I first heard about this, from my old classmate Nicky D'Eon at the grocery store, I assumed it was a joke. But then I took a selfie down in the city using FlashCapture, and an Achievement burst across the screen.

"Congratulations. You've snapped one of the most reclusive and mysterious inhabitants of the City Beneath. The Hermit discovered the city in '06 and has been at the top of the FlashCapture leaderboards since the creation of this app. Can you beat her high score?"

Needless to say, this pissed me off. I emailed Dan, but he said his hands were tied, that he no longer made the decisions at FlashCapture. He had sold his share the previous year and was no longer on the board.

* * *

It was around that time that the ghosts began to disappear. At first, there were fewer and fewer ghosts clustered around the bridges and the main levels. On the main message boards, Spookheads complained that it was getting harder and harder for newbies to break into the game. You could easily spend a whole day down there and only see Howlers and Winders with no Rares at all. After a while, day-trippers were spotting nothing but Winders. By the end of the year, they were spotting nothing at all.

People complained that you had to explore for at least three days if you wanted to capture anything. Then a week. Then even the most die-hard explorers failed to see anything at all.

Interest in the app began to taper off. It got disappointing reviews, and think pieces were written about how the craze was over. Stock prices plunged.

And so the Invisibles were born. They called it FlashCapture 2.0. With a single update, the City Beneath was full of ghosts once more. Except you couldn't see these ghosts with your naked eye. You could only see them on the screen of your smartphone. Kids these days are skeptical that you ever *could* see the ghosts.

A lot of people think it was the update that drove me away. In the popular imagination, I was disgusted by the very idea of the Invisibles. I admit that I encouraged that belief. But it wasn't true.

With Invisibles, FlashCapture could control the distribution and frequency of the ghosts, letting them create tutorials for newcomers, clever challenges for veteran Spookheads. They could ensure a satisfying payoff at the end of every trip—a beautiful, crafted climax that made the expense worth it. They even invented new ghosts to find. I'm certain Crushers, Meatheads, and Lollygaggers didn't exist before the update.

The Spookheads loved it.

Version 2.0 was a bright new dawn for the City Beneath. They said that the move to Invisibles took "courage," as if it had been the company's idea to do away with the real ghosts. They called Dan a visionary, even though he swore to me that he wasn't involved. They said it was better than the old version by a million miles.

And do you want to hear something terrible? They were right. I tried it out, and I was immediately hooked. The app knew all the places I had been. It knew I had captured more ghosts than anyone else. And it made life in the City Beneath exciting again. I found a new Invisible on the first day, and the app fed me clues about where I would find more. It generated little points of light in the air, like bread crumbs. It made me want to explore. It made me want to defend my turf at the top of the leaderboard. With the new Invisibles, others were creeping up on my high score.

So I started exploring again. I moved deeper into the city, to side chambers that only I knew about. They were empty to the naked eye, but when I raised my phone, they were full of wonder.

So why did I leave? Why did I move away from Yarmouth and never return? I left because of Johnny Grayson. I followed a bread-crumb trail through a slanting tunnel in the lower depths. I found him limping through the darkness, with his broken foot and leather jacket. I'm the only user to have spotted him. He's an UltraRare, so he doesn't appear on any of the leaderboards. He doesn't even appear on the Wiki. As far as I know, I'm the only one to have seen him, so the only evidence of his existence is on my phone (and, I suppose, on some FlashCapture server somewhere). But he exists. The app knew who he was immediately. Johnny Grayson. An UltraRare.

He glowed faintly on the screen for a few moments before limping away from me. And when I lowered my phone, he was no longer there. And I never returned to the City Beneath and its ghosts.

The Surface of the Moon

WE FELL ASLEEP UNDER THE MIDNIGHT SUN BUT WOKE UP ON the surface of the Moon.

We knew we were no longer on Devon Island, because we could see stars. It had been a summer of endless light. The sun was like a nervous swimmer, splashing in the shallows of the horizon but never quite taking the plunge. A seductive golden dusk took the place of night, setting the rhythm of those days, letting us know we had stayed up too late yet again. With our parents gone, bedtimes were a thing of the past. It made for late starts, but that didn't worry us anymore. Without the deadline of darkness, we could afford to dawdle. What did it matter if we reached our next waypoint in the middle of the night? There would always be enough light to make camp by. More importantly, there was no one else around, and solitude gave us the luxury of sloppiness. We liked to pretend we were the only two people left alive. Maybe we were.

Be we woke that night to galaxies burning overhead. A lifeless lunar landscape awaited us. We burst from the air lock of our tent, barefoot and laughing, leaving pristine prints in the fine gray sand. Those prints would remain perfect forever in the vacuum of space without breezes to dull their edges and fill their hollows. This would have been an unthinkable risk back on Earth, but here on the Moon we could leave tracks without fear of pursuit.

We went bounding across the silent desert in our pajamas, each step enormous and effortless. There was no trace of that delicious ache that usually settled in our muscles while we slept. Without our packs to drag us down, we were almost weightless. Everything felt buoyant, even our cheeks. It was impossible not to grin.

The lack of oxygen was not a concern, for we had the Moon in our blood. As little children, we had been accused of mooning about, wasting our time on silly fantasies. But those countless hours of make-believe sustained us in this impossible landscape, just as they had sustained us through the Bad Days back home, before we came north. We had plenty of practice surviving without space suits on distant planets and battling moon monsters with our bare hands. When our parents told us to hide, we hid from aliens in the craters of other worlds. When they told us to run, we ran with rockets in our heels. These were our old stomping grounds, as familiar and alien as anywhere on Earth. In many ways, we were more adapted to this environment than we were to home.

* * *

Before the Warmth came, Mom told us about the way life would be once we reached the Moon. We wouldn't be able to go outside, she said, and we'd live with lots of other people in a small dome. But we'd be safe from the Warmth. The sun's rays would bounce right off the silver surface and scatter back into space without an atmosphere to trap them.

When Dad went out foraging and did not return, Mom pulled us close and told us we must become moons ourselves. She told us to let the bad feelings bounce off and scatter harmlessly away. It was OK to feel sad or afraid, she said, but if we trapped those feelings in our atmosphere, the Warmth would come for us too.

* * *

Later, she told us we were her moons, that we would always be in her orbit. That was just before the Warmth came for her.

It was cold there on the Moon. It was a delicious, rare feeling that flooded my senses. I wanted to pull off my pajamas and bathe in it.

But there was also a nervous edge to it that made me want to curl up and cry.

The next day, we would wake up on Earth once more, the Moon low on the horizon, distant and ghostly in the blue of the morning sky. We would linger over our hot chocolate, not speaking. And as we laced up our boots, we would feel the fine moon dust in the cracks between our toes and remember where we had been.

*   *   *

Our first glimpse of the Haughton Lunar Analog Research Station felt like violence. It was bright, garish, and angular after the countless days we'd spent trudging across the gentle swells and empty horizons of Devon Island's gray plains. Quonset huts huddled around the main building, a geodesic dome with the flags of Canada and the United States and Nunavut and NASA and the ESA emblazoned on the side. There was a solar-generating plant and a greenhouse and big tanks that said OXYGEN and PROPANE and HYDROGEN on the sides. A couple of rusty Humvees sat nearby, like enormous snails.

We stopped for a few hours to watch for signs of life from a distance, just like we had promised Mom we would. But our hearts weren't in it. We knew there was no one there. And even if there had been, how would that have changed anything? We couldn't just turn around.

Without speaking, we nodded to each other and jogged down the gentle slope, leaving our packs behind.

*   *   *

They'd originally chosen this crater as a place to prepare for a mission to Mars. But as humanity's horizons narrowed, as every test rocket made things worse, they grew less ambitious. The Moon would do. That's when Mom first came here in a Twin Otter with a dozen other scientists. She returned to us after three months, energized and full of hope. It was the first time we had seen her hopeful about anything. But then the Bad Days began. And that was when our horizons narrowed even more. It wouldn't be a new start for humanity on another world. It wouldn't even be a lunar enclave for the ultrawealthy. It would just be us, living alone in a place that pretended to be anywhere but

Earth. It was a place with airtight walls and solar panels and all the necessary supplies to last a lifetime. A place built to pretend the air was unbreathable and the temperature intolerable. A place that pretended hard enough.

* * *

The first damage we noticed was to the greenhouse. Several of the panes were smashed, and all the plants inside were rotting. Mom told us the solar station should still be running, that we should be able to hear the hum of electricity. But it was silent and dead. She had given us the emergency override code for the air lock, but we didn't need it. A great ragged gash had been cut in the side of the dome. That dome that was supposed to keep out the Warmth was open to the atmosphere.

We held hands as we stepped into the dark interior. Everything was a mess. The freezers sat lifeless. The pantry was empty. The lifetime of provisions that Mom had told us about was gone. There was no power, and everything stank of mold.

It didn't feel like tragedy, even after a thousand miles of walking toward this place. We were moons. Our atmospheres were too thin to trap disappointment. Instead, we rummaged through the closets and pulled out the gleaming space suits. They were heavy and way too big, but we climbed into them anyway and stumbled out of the air lock onto the surface of the Moon, where there were always stars overhead and the Warmth would never reach.

ACKNOWLEDGMENTS

MANY THANKS TO MICHELLE PRETORIUS AND *INDIANA Review* for choosing this collection for the 2020 Blue Light Books Prize and to the team at Indiana University Press for making it a reality.

I would also like to thank the many people who supported and inspired me while I wrote the stories in this collection.

Thank you to Sean Michaels, Anca Szilágyi, and Jordan Himmelfarb for your support and inspiration when we were all fledgling writers in Montreal. Thank you for helping me hone my craft and for showing me what was possible.

Special thanks to Cecil Day for granting us permission to use your art on the cover, to Sarah Jevnikar for your insight into the assistive technologies mentioned in *The Visible Spectrum*, and to Michael R. Burch for granting us permission to use your translation of Kobayashi Issa's haiku, which inspired *The World of Dew*.

Thank you to my friends and collaborators in Yarmouth—Adam Graham, Sherrie Graham, James Turpin, Jordan Muise, Ian Travis, Glence Glasgow, Melanie Cotter, Mark Palmer, Sarah Fells, Ashley Nickerson, Shawn Cottreau, Stephanie Welton, Andrew Welton, James Condon, Sacha Begg, Ryan Muise, Shirleen Atkinson, Gordon Rothwell, Cecil Day, and everyone else who helps make our little town a hotbed of creativity and kindness. I wrote these stories fueled by your friendship.

Thank you to my mum, Louise Mortimer, for nurturing my earliest storytelling and introducing me to the works of Mervyn Peake and Ursula K. Le Guin. To my dad, Arnold Smith, for teaching me to believe in magic and aliens and dreams. To my brothers, Daniel Smith and Henry Smith, for your creativity, curiosity, and courage. And to all four of you for your love, of course.

Finally, thank you to Megan Snow and Owen Snowsmith for more than I could ever hope to express. Together, we're living the best of all possible lives.

CREDITS

The following stories originally appeared in these publications:

"Come-from-Aways." *Asimov's Science Fiction*. December 2015.
"Barb-the-Bomb and the Yesterday Boy." *Daily Science Fiction*. May 5, 2011.
"The World of Dew." *Pulp Literature*. Fall 2015.
"Professor Jennifer Magda-Chichester's Time Machine." *Daily Science Fiction*. September 2012.
"The Fumblers Alley Risk Emporium." *Urban Fantasy Magazine*. December 2014.
"The Mugger's Hymn." *AE: The Canadian Science Fiction Review*. November 2012.
"Joey LeRath's Rocket Ship." *Daily Science Fiction*. February 2012.
"The Washerwoman and the Troll." *Andromeda Spaceways Inflight Magazine*. May 2013.
"Headshot." *Terraform*. March 2015.
"The Visible Spectrum." *AE: The Canadian Science Fiction Review*. September 2011.
"Hospice." *Daily Science Fiction*. August 2015.
"Practice." *AE: The Canadian Science Fiction Review*. September 2015.
"The Monster." *Daily Science Fiction*. October 2016.

Julian Mortimer Smith is a writer of speculative fiction. His short stories have appeared in many of the world's top science fiction and fantasy venues, including *Asimov's, Lightspeed, Terraform,* and *Best American Science Fiction and Fantasy.* He lives in Yarmouth, Nova Scotia, Canada.

CPSIA information can be obtained
at www.ICGtesting.com
Printed in the USA
LVHW072337221121
704127LV00023B/401